PRAISE FOR T.

"Dive in…if you are looking to be charmed and delighted."

LOCUS

"…[A] knack for creating colorful, instantly memorable characters, and inhuman creatures capable of inspiring awe and wonder."

NPR BOOKS

"The writing. It is superb. T. Kingfisher, where have you been all my life?"

THE BOOK SMUGGLERS

"…you walk away going 'Damn, that was good but there's a new layer of trauma living inside me.'"

KB SPANGLER, DIGITAL DIVIDE

ILLUMINATIONS

T. KINGFISHER

Illuminations
Ebook by Red Wombat Studio
Print edition copyright © 2022 Argyll Productions
Copyright © 2022 by T. Kingfisher
http://www.tkingfisher.com

Published by Argyll Productions
Dallas, Texas
www.argyllproductions.com

Print ISBN: 978-1-61450-577-8
eBook ISBN: 978-1-61450-578-5

First Edition Paperback November 2022

ONE

Morning
Garlic Day
Messidor, the Month of Harvest

ONCE UPON A TIME, there was a girl named Rosa. She had
black hair and brown skin and brown eyes and she was a little
bit plump and her favorite color was purple and she was
deeply, profoundly, exquisitely *bored.*

"I am more bored than anyone has ever been in the history
of the world," she said, lying on her back on her bed and staring
at the distant ceiling. "However bored anyone has ever been, I
am a hundred times more bored than that."

She was talking out loud to a painting. The painting didn't
say anything, but then, Rosa didn't expect it to. It was not a

very good painting, but Rosa was not a very good painter. At least, not yet.

She lived in the world-famous Studio Mandolini, home to the Mandolini family, the greatest painters of magical illuminations in the city. If you wanted a magical illumination—a painting that would carry a magical charm—you went to the Studio Mandolini and told them what you wanted, and they would paint it.

Rosa was extremely proud of her family, even if they weren't doing anything to stop her from dying of boredom.

The Mandolinis painted pictures of radishes with wings to ward off sickness, and they painted great droopy-faced hounds with halos to protect against burglars. They painted flaming swords on shingles to keep storms from blowing the roofs off houses, and they painted very strange pictures of men with hummingbird heads to keep venomous snakes out of people's gardens.

And every one of these paintings worked, although they would wear out over time. Sometimes the illumination had to be very large. It was no good getting a tiny painting of a blue-eyed cat to keep mice away if you had a barn that was already full of rats. The tiny painting would keep mice out of your pantry, but to keep them out of a barn, you needed a painting six feet high with a blue-eyed cat the size of a tiger.

It could be any sort of cat in any kind of position, but it had to have blue eyes. Illuminations were very specific that way. It didn't matter if your favorite color was purple—if you snuck into the pantry and painted the cat's eyes purple, it would stop working and mice would come in and dance all over the cheese.

(Rosa had been very young when she gave the cat in the

pantry purple eyes, and her grandmother had forgiven her for it, even though they had to throw out all the cheese.)

She was five years older now—ten, nearly eleven, and a great deal wiser than when she was five, nearly six. She understood all about illuminations and how you never *ever* changed them. And that was the problem.

It was very boring, when you wanted to draw, to always have to draw the same things the same way. Maybe you didn't *want* the man to have a hummingbird's head. Maybe you wanted him to have a crocodile's head so he could open his mouth very wide and swallow up your chores.

Maybe you wanted the cats to have purple eyes, or green eyes, or one green eye and one purple eye.

Maybe you wanted to paint radishes with teeth instead of wings.

The problem was that if you painted it that way, the magic wouldn't work. And the Studio Mandolini was famous for the fact that their illuminations *always* worked.

Rosa loved her two uncles and her aunt and her cousin and her grandmother, who made up the Studio Mandolini. She loved them all very much and they had taken very good care of her. Her parents had died so long ago that Rosa could barely remember them, but her family at the Studio Mandolini was wonderful.

They did not always understand about Rosa's paintings, though.

"That's very interesting," said Uncle Marco, when she showed him her radish with teeth. "But isn't it supposed to have wings?"

"Needs wings," said her Cousin Sergio, who talked in very short sentences, as if he was afraid he would run out of words.

He was only twenty-five, but he was already losing his hair. "Won't sell. No wings."

"Interesting modern primitivist technique," said her Aunt Nadia, who was very thin and wore black and talked about art history a lot. "I see what you're trying to do, subverting the very *nature* of illumination making. But I don't think the art world is *ready*, Rosa. You are too far ahead of your time."

Rosa didn't want to be ahead of her time. She wanted to be an illumination painter. But the radishes didn't do anything. She could feel that there was something to them—something that was *almost* magic, but not quite—but that didn't matter. People wanted the real thing.

"It's lovely," said Uncle Alfonso. "It's *art,* that's what it is. Not stuffy illuminations. That's a different sort of magic." And he took a pin and put Rosa's radish up on the wall of his studio, where he put all the things that interested him, like drawings of hands and woodpecker feathers and an empty turtle shell and oak leaves with big spotted puffballs on them.

Uncle Alfonso was her very favorite relative. He was actually a great uncle, or an uncle once removed. Rosa wasn't quite sure how it worked. (He was also even older than Grandmama, because people had very big families in those days and Grandmama's brother had started having children before Grandmama's mother had quite finished, so Uncle Alfonso had been born six months before his own aunt.)

Uncle Alfonso always called her "Rosalita" which meant "little rose" and no one was allowed to call her that but him.

Even if they didn't always understand about her radishes, her family was very nice. Dinner time was always loud and everyone laughed a great deal and told stories and jokes and no one was allowed to talk about sad things because, as Grandmama said, it would upset the digestion. There was actually an illumination painted on the table, of two peppermills crossed like swords, to prevent indigestion and queasiness and upset stomach, but Grandmama Mandolini did not believe in taking chances.

She loved her family, and she could not imagine living anywhere other than the Studio Mandolini.

But her family was also very busy, because they were the very best in the world, and so when Rosa was bored, she had to find ways to entertain herself.

TWO

THE STUDIO MANDOLINI was very tall and had windows all the way up to the ceiling, to let in the light that was so essential for painting. The ground floor was cut up into little rooms, called "bays," but none of the bays had ceilings. Everyone had their own walls and their own personal workspace and a bedroom behind the workspace, up against the wall.

Rosa had slept for a long time on the couch in Grandmama's room, but when she turned nine, she was given her very own bay in the studio. It was a little bit bare, because everyone else had big stacks of canvases and wooden boards to paint on, and Rosa had only a pad of paper and a pencil and lots of drawings of radishes, but it was her very own. Uncle Alfonso had given her an interesting owl feather, which she had tacked up on the wall next to her very best radish drawing. Aunt Nadia had painted an illumination to ward away nightmares, of a cheerful little pig surrounded by flames. (The flames did not seem to be bothering the pig at all.) Rosa put it up over her bed and whenever she did not have a nightmare, she thought very kindly of Aunt Nadia.

It was not quite perfect. At night, she could hear Cousin Sergio snoring in his bay next to hers, and sometimes, when his allergies were bothering him, Uncle Alfonso would snore too and Rosa would have to put a pillow over her head to drown them all out. Usually, though, it was pretty good.

But not today. Today, rain was coming down gray and drizzly against the enormous studio windows and Rosa was as bored as she had ever been in her life.

She had drawn radishes until she was tired of them. Some had teeth and some had claws and some breathed fire, but none of them had wings.

She had read all her books, several times over.

She had tried to write a story, but she couldn't think of what the story should be about, so she added in a monster to come and eat the hero. She wrote "The End" and signed her name, but while this was somewhat satisfying, it was also only six lines long and she still had the rest of the afternoon left to go.

"I'm bored," she told Cousin Sergio.

"Can't talk!" he said. "Painting! Nearly done!"

"I'm bored," she told Uncle Marco.

"Hmm," said Uncle Marco. "Interesting."

"No," said Rosa. "It's not. If it were interesting, I wouldn't be bored. Being bored is the *opposite* of interesting."

Uncle Marco pushed his glasses up on his nose. "You could go play outside."

"It's raining."

"Rain is *very* interesting."

Rosa gave up and went to the next bay.

She gave Aunt Nadia's studio a very wide berth because Aunt Nadia was doing a big painting for the Merchant's Guild, which required eleven angels holding various objects, and which was supposed to ward off bribery and corruption and also termites. Aunt Nadia liked to work from live models if she could, and if Rosa went into the studio, she would undoubtedly be dressed up in angel robes and told to hold very still.

Rosa didn't mind modeling for paintings. She had done it lots of times. There was an illumination on the wall of the grocery to keep food from spoiling that was actually a painting of Rosa as a baby. Rosa always felt smug when she went into the grocery and saw it there.

Sitting still for hours was surprisingly hard, though. You started to get stiff in muscles that you didn't even know existed. You got breaks every few minutes, but the rest of the time you had to sit absolutely still and not whine and not fidget. If you moved even a little, the artist had to either change the painting or rush over and move you back to the way you had been and it was all a great deal more difficult than anyone who hadn't done it would think.

So she snuck past Aunt Nadia's bay, feeling just a tiny bit guilty.

Uncle Alfonso had gone out to buy paint, and that left only Grandmama Mandolini.

Grandmama was bent over a ledger, making sure that the studio accounts balanced. It was not the sort of thing that a ten-year-old could help with, even if she was nearly eleven.

"I'm boooooorrred," announced Rosa.

"Go play with Serena," said Grandmama, not taking her eyes off the ledger.

Rosa scowled. "I don't always like Serena," she said.

"Nonsense," said Grandmama. "You're best friends, or you were last week. Go play."

Rosa heaved a great sigh, but there was no arguing with that tone of voice. She put on her shoes and picked up an umbrella and went to go play with Serena.

SERENA LIVED THREE BLOCKS AWAY, on the main street, instead of at the end of a higgledy-piggledy alleyway. Her family were illumination painters too, but not as talented or as famous as Studio Mandolini.

Rosa had been telling the exact truth when she said that she didn't always like Serena. She wasn't entirely sure that she liked her right now, but at least walking to Serena's house would give her something to do.

Serena was a year and a bit older and had just turned twelve. They had been thrown together for years, because even very sensible grown-ups seem to believe that children will be friends simply because they are the same age.

When they had been younger, they would play together, and Serena would always say, "You have to do what I say, because I'm older!"

It was some years before Rosa realized that Serena would always be older, and there was never going to be a time when they did what Rosa wanted. This seemed very unfair.

("Life isn't fair," Aunt Nadia said, when Rosa told her this. "But she'll probably die first, being older, so it works out." This was *not* the sort of comfort that Rosa was looking for. Aunt Nadia was bad with children, and even worse with adults.)

When they were young, they had pretended to be horses, which was fine, or Great Beauties, which was...less fine. You could usually insert a monster into a story about horses, but not one about Great Beauties.

"We'll be Great Beauties, "said Serena. "We'll take the town by storm and go to the opera and the theater and everyone will be dying to be seen with us. And I'm the prettiest."

"Then I'm the smartest," said Rosa.

"Then I'm the most fashionable," said Serena.

"And I'm the bravest," said Rosa.

Serena scowled. "You don't need to be *bravest*," she said.

"What if there are monsters?"

"There aren't any monsters in this story."

"There could be a *little* monster?" said Rosa hopefully. "At the opera, maybe? It could come into our box at the opera and you can swoon very prettily and people will fan you and bring you lemon ices and I will kick the monster in the head with my boots."

"Great Beauties don't wear *boots* to the *opera*," said Serena darkly.

"I'm not the fashionable one," said Rosa. "So I've got boots."

"You're such a *child*," said Serena, and refused to play anymore.

It didn't help that Serena was very pretty, with deep amber skin and hair like black silk, and that she was already nearly four inches taller than Rosa.

Lately Serena had stopped saying, "You have to do what I say!" and had started rolling her eyes and saying, "You'll understand when you're *older*," as if an extra year was a brick wall thirty feet high and Rosa was on the wrong side of it. And she frequently didn't want to play any games at all, but instead wanted to talk about boys that she thought were handsome. Rosa was skeptical of this, because Uncle Marco said that beautiful people were boring to paint and that normal people, who had bumps and wrinkles and folds, were much more interesting. Being interesting seemed like a much better deal than being handsome, but that only made Serena roll her eyes harder.

But despite all this, sometimes they were still friends, and Serena and Rosa would lay on the floor of Serena's bedroom and draw pictures. Serena drew horses and unicorns and gryphons and Rosa drew horses and monsters and fanged radishes. Those were pretty good times. Serena's horses were better—Rosa had a hard time getting the hind legs right—but Rosa's monsters were bigger and had more teeth and fangs and eyeballs and whiskers.

And they never argued about the future—the *real* future, not the pretend one where they were beauties and the toast of the town. The real future, they both knew, was that they would learn the family trade and become illuminators and spend their lives painting in the studios where they had grown up.

THREE

Afternoon
Garlic Day
Messidor, the Month of Harvest

ROSA TURNED down the street where Serena lived. You could see her family's studio right away, because it had a portico, like an archway with columns. You couldn't possibly miss it.

There were gold letters over the grand portico, proclaiming it the home of the Studio Magnifico. Rosa ignored it and went to the smaller entrance next door. Serena's family didn't sleep in their studios the way that Rosa's did. They had ordinary bedrooms and weren't surrounded by canvases all the time.

("Strange way for an artist to live," Uncle Marco had said, when Rosa told him that. "How can you make art when you aren't breathing it in while you dream?")

"Hush," said Uncle Alfonso. "All artists are different. As long as what they are doing works for them, it is no business of ours to say it's wrong."

Rosa said nothing, but she was secretly proud of the fact that the Mandolinis slept in their studios and dreamed with their art. It was one more thing that made the Studio Mandolini special, and just a little bit better than the Studio Magnifico. Not that Serena would ever admit it.)

The sidewalks here weren't full of cracks and loose cobblestones, the way they were in Rosa's neighborhood. You could still smell the canal, though. No matter how rich a neighborhood was, you couldn't get away from the city's canals. In high summer, when the smell was worst, they usually went to Rosa's house because it was in an older neighborhood and had been placed farther away from the water. Most of the time, though, Serena insisted they draw at the Studio Magnifico, because her bedroom was bigger than Rosa's bay and the floors were soft carpet instead of hard tile.

Rosa knocked on the house door and waited.

Serena's brother came to the door. He looked down at Rosa —he was very tall—and said, "Oh, it's you."

"Is Serena home?" asked Rosa. Serena's brother was seventeen and almost a grown-up. He had been working at the Studio Magnifico for two years now.

"Sure," he said, holding the door open. He turned and yelled "Serena!" over his shoulder. "*Serena!* Someone's here for you!"

Serena appeared in the doorway a moment later. Her face fell when she saw Rosa, and Rosa couldn't help but feel like Serena had been expecting to see someone else.

"Oh, it's you," she said, in a rather nastier tone than her

brother had used. "I don't have time to play with you, Rosa. I have a *commission*."

Rosa's eyebrows shot up. "A commission?" she said. "*You've got a commission?*" (A commission was when a customer came to the studio and gave the painters money to make an illumination. Rosa saw it happen all the time at the studio, but had never imagined that someone would commission a twelve-year-old.)

"Of course," said Serena. "I'm an illumination painter, you know." She lifted her chin.

"Yeah, but you're a kid," said Rosa. "Nobody commissions *kids*."

Serena flushed. "I am *twelve*," she said angrily. "And I *do* have a commission, because everybody knows that the Studio Magnifico are the best painters in the city, no matter how old we are!"

Rosa blinked. Serena had never said anything like that before, and so Rosa didn't have time to think of a better reply than, "But the Mandolinis..."

"Nobody wants Mandolini commissions any more. You're too weird and old-fashioned."

Finally, Rosa managed to say, "We are *not*," but it sounded small and weak and much too late.

"You *are*. Our family is going to leave yours in the *dust*." And she stomped away, leaving Rosa very startled on the doorstep.

Her brother caught the door before it slammed shut. "Don't listen to her," he told Rosa. "The café down the street wants illuminations on all their jar lids to keep the grain moths out. It's twenty-seven drawings of gryphons holding acorns, that's all."

"She draws really good gryphons," said Rosa glumly.

"Yeah," said her brother, "but to hear her talk, she's got a commission to paint charms on the Dynast's lapdog's collar. Don't worry about it." He waved to Rosa and shut the door.

Rosa walked back home, dragging her feet.

"We're *not* weird," she said angrily, under her breath. "And we *are* the best."

Admittedly, she was talking to herself, and maybe that was a little bit weird, but it was because she was angry, not because she was a Mandolini. Mandolinis weren't weird. Mandolinis were amazing and talented and everybody knew they were the best illumination painters in the city.

She couldn't believe that Serena had a commission, though. Even if it was just drawing gryphons on jar lids.

Her shoulders sagged as she walked. *She* didn't have a commission. She didn't have any jobs to do. Nobody wanted her to draw fanged radishes for them. Fanged radishes didn't actually do anything. They weren't a proper illumination at all.

She knew that she shouldn't be jealous of Serena. You weren't supposed to be jealous of your friends. *Although after what Serena said, maybe we aren't friends after all.*

Boredom started to settle over her again, like a dull beige cloud. Now it was even worse, because it was mixed with a feeling that if she were better or older or just somehow *more,* she would have something to do.

It was bad enough being bored. Being bored and inadequate was nearly unbearable.

If I was older, I'd draw illuminations. Real ones. I'd have real commissions and everything.

She didn't let herself think about the alternative. Not every Mandolini became an illuminator. Grandmama didn't have the gift for magic, and even though she ran everything and the studio would fall apart without her, Rosa didn't want to be like that. She wanted to be an illuminator.

But even when she drew everything exactly right, according to the books, it didn't become an illumination. Not quite. Sometimes there was a little bit of magic in it, but not enough.

Not like Serena's gryphons.

Rosa let herself into the studio and closed the door, setting her back against it. She sighed from the bottom of her toes.

Light streamed from the last bay. Her favorite uncle was home.

FOUR

Evening
Garlic Day
Messidor, the Month of Harvest

"Serena said something strange," she told Uncle Alfonso, flinging herself into the overstuffed chair in his studio. The cushions made a very satisfying THWUMPH sound when she landed on them.

Uncle Alfonso gazed at his painting, holding his brush in the air. "Ah?" he said, sounding somewhat distracted.

Rosa poured out the story of what happened, except for the fact that she hadn't been able to think of anything to say but, "We are *not*."

"And Serena has a *commission*," she finished, trying not to sound as aggrieved as she really felt.

"Good for her," said Uncle Alfonso. "I'm sure she'll do well."

Rosa scowled. If Uncle Alfonso had a flaw, it was that he always saw the best in people and was happy for everyone.

"But it's not *true*, is it? That we're old-fashioned and weird?"

Uncle Alfonso considered this. He considered it for so long that Rosa started to get a tense knot in her stomach. "Uncle?"

"Well," he said. "It's true that we're not as popular as we used to be. The Mandolinis have a particular style, you know, and tastes change. People want different things. And there aren't as many of us as there used to be, so we can't always keep up with commissions." He placed a careful stroke on the painting. "We are not quite where we used to be."

Rosa felt the knot in her stomach drawing tighter. "But...we still get commissions, don't we?"

"Oh, yes," said Uncle Alfonso. "Enough to keep the studio going. And your Aunt Nadia has a commission for the Merchant's Guild and when it is done, they will pay us a great deal of money. And many influential people will see it, and perhaps they will want one like it."

He looked over from the painting and smiled at her. "It will be all right, Rosalita. Have faith."

Rosa wiggled her fingers. Her stomach felt a little better, but not completely. "Is there an illumination to make people like art?"

"An illumination to make people like art..." He made a delicate little brush stroke on the painting, adding a white highlight to a painted tomato. "Now that is a good question, Rosalita." He pursed his lips. "Things that change people's moods are hard. You should check the Codex."

Rosa slid out of the chair and went to go find the Codex.

There were two books in the studio of any illumination painter. One was the great *Codex Iconographica* and one was the *Iconographer's Concordance*.

Both of them were enormous and weighed twenty pounds each. Rosa grabbed the Codex and staggered back to the chair. The book was as big as her torso, and she spread it open over her lap.

The Codex was an alphabetical listing, rather like a dictionary. Instead of definitions, it had descriptions of illuminations. If you looked up the word *mice*, for example:

Mice
To ward off: blue-eyed cat, any species

To attract: round ball of cheese

To keep healthy: mouse-headed man with the crescent moon under his feet

---

And by this you would know what to paint in order to get the proper effect, whether you were trying to bring mice to you or keep them away or keep a pet mouse healthy.

(In truth, there was only so much you could do with the wards to keep animals or people healthy. If the mouse was already sick, an illumination couldn't fix it, and if the mouse wasn't being fed properly or was old or its cage was drafty, the mouse would get sick eventually, even if you put an illumination over its cage. Illuminations wore out quickly if you asked them to do impossible things. Even the radishes with wings that the Studio Mandolini sold only made sickness less likely. They could not banish it entirely.)

Rosa flipped through the Codex to the L section.

She found illuminations for warding off lions and for keeping lice away, and to prevent lasagna from getting mushy, but nothing to make people like art. Then it occurred to her that she was looking things up wrong, and switched to A, but the section for *Art* was sixteen pages long, in very small print, and she gave up after two pages.

"Well," said Uncle Alfonso, dabbing more paint on his brush. "It's hard to change people's moods, as I said. Too close to changing minds, and that's forbidden."

"I thought we could do an illumination to make people like *our* art," said Rosa.

"Mmm." Uncle Alfonso shook his head. "Too dangerous. Where do you stop, Rosalita? What if someone wanted to change your mind so you *wanted* to do your chores? Or to love squash?"

Rosa stuck her tongue out. "Yuck."

"Yes, but you'd love it. You wouldn't have any choice. And in very little time, maybe we'd paint so many illuminations to change you that you wouldn't be *you* any more, and then who would you be?"

"We'd only use the one," said Rosa. "A small one."

Uncle Alfonso raised an eyebrow. "And then your friend Serena's family does a bigger one, so that people like their art better. And then the Studio Lasrina across town paints one as big as a ceiling. Best not to start, I think."

Rosa shut the Codex with a thump. "Okay," she said. "Maybe that isn't a good idea. Is there something else I can do to help?"

"To help?"

"You know." Rosa wiggled her fingers. "To help the family. I can't make a painting for the Merchant's Guild. I mean, unless they want radishes."

"I am quite fond of your radishes, Rosalita."

"Yeah, but you're my uncle. You *have* to like them."

Uncle Alfonso smiled. "You put your heart into them. That's what matters. Every illumination takes a piece of the painter's heart, and that is why the magic works."

Rosa scowled. "Doesn't that mean I'll run out of heart if I draw too many?"

"Fortunately," said Uncle Alfonso, "you are still quite young. Your heart is growing so fast that you cannot possibly run out. In fact, it is probably wise if you draw as much as possible to keep it from exploding."

She stuck her tongue out at him. "My heart isn't going to explode!"

"Probably not," said Uncle Alfonso, "but there is no sense in taking chances." He dabbed another stroke on the painting. "If you want to help, why don't you go into the basement?"

"What's in the basement?"

"Everything. Go poke around. But particularly look for the stuffed armadillo, and if you find it, bring it up. I need to paint an illumination to ward away blisters, and I've misplaced the armadillo."

Stuffed armadillos were quite interesting, and searching for one meant she was doing something useful, even if it wasn't as useful as taking a commission of her own. Rosa slid off the chair and went in search of the missing armadillo.

FIVE

THE BASEMENT of the Studio Mandolini had dozens of rooms. The rooms were full of closets and all the rooms and all the closets were full of trunks and boxes and fascinating junk. Whenever one of the Mandolinis needed a model for a particular illumination, they would get it out of the basement, and whenever they finished painting that particular illumination, they would shove the model back in the basement.

There were fabulous costumes for people to wear and stuffed animals with glass eyes—not like Rosa's favorite stuffed bear, but real animals that had once been alive and had been mounted on plaques after they died. There were props for the human models to hold, like swords and shields and spears, and props for them to wear, like crowns and tiaras and suits of armor.

Mostly, however, there were boxes and boxes and boxes of junk. The artists were often very bad about labeling things, so there was no telling where anything actually was. You could find a dagger shoved carelessly into a bowl of wax fruit and a stuffed wombat wedged into a trunk full of crowns.

It was a glorious muddle.

Rosa rolled up her sleeves and began hunting armadillos.

She found boxes of candles and boxes of feathers and boxes holding other boxes. She opened dusty trunks full of dusty clothes. She pulled down hatboxes that held fabulous hats, and hatboxes that held jumbles of shoes and a hatbox that was full of old paper wasp nests. She found stuffed ducks and stuffed weasels and an enormous moth-eaten stuffed heron holding a fish in its beak, which Cousin Sergio had been looking for only last week.

She did not find the armadillo.

"Someday, someone must organize this," said Rosa grimly. It was something her grandmother said regularly, and something Uncle Alfonso said as well. Sergio had yelled it while he was looking for the heron: "Must organize! Too messy!"

Aunt Nadia had waved a languid hand and said, "Why don't we just knock the building down? Then we can start over from scratch with proper labels this time."

Grandmama had given Aunt Nadia a *look* for that, and Nadia had ducked her head and grinned.

Well, if I never learn how to make illuminations, I could make it my life's work to clean the basement. That would be helpful for everybody. And I might finish before I die of old age.

She looked over the sea of boxes.

...or I might expire dramatically in a pile of stuffed badgers. She imagined herself, white-haired and older than Uncle Alfonso, having a dramatic death scene in the basement.

Rosa clutched her chest, reeled, gasped out, "Tell them...I died...for art..." and flung herself backwards onto boxes. Then she giggled, which she probably wouldn't do if she was dead. Serena would have told her to hush, that corpses don't giggle.

She had to give Serena credit: Serena loved a good death scene as much as Rosa did. She generally wanted to die of consumption or unrequited love, though, while Rosa preferred to be eaten by monsters. But once you were dying, you got to gasp out your last words and fall over, and that was always fun.

Serena's last words were usually "Tell them—I died—for love—!" Rosa's last words were often "Arrrrrgh it hurts, the pain, the pain, why did the monster eat my legs!?"

Then the other girl would hum the funeral march and throw fake rose petals until the dead one giggled too much to stay properly dead. This was all enormously satisfying.

Rosa climbed out of the badger pile and looked around. There was

a gap between boxes that led into the most crowded room of all. It was too small for a grown-up to get through, but Rosa wiggled sideways until she fit. Trunks and suitcases were piled up to the ceiling and she had to climb a pile of boxes like a ladder to get into the back.

There was a closet door back there, with a label on the door that said "More Stuff."

This was not helpful at all.

An armadillo probably counts as "stuff," Rosa thought. *At least, it's stuffed, and things that are stuffed are definitely stuff.*

The hinges squealed when she pulled the door open.

Six bolts of lace fell out. They had been white once, but were yellow with age. A calendar fell down with them, and when she picked it up, the cover said "CORONATION EDITION!"

Rosa considered this.

She had learned in school, just last week, that the Dynast of the city had been crowned thirty-two years ago. The ceremony was called a coronation. That meant the calendar was thirty-two years old.

It occurred to Rosa that no one had opened this closet since long before she was born.

She shoved the bolts of lace aside, propping them up against the wall, and peered into the closet.

On the shelf in front of her, just at eye level, there was a wooden box about two feet long and eight inches high. It was propped up at an angle so that the lid faced her.

The lid was dusty, but she could see painted figures through it. Rosa pulled down her sleeve and wiped it over the lid.

The picture was of a crow. It had brilliantly painted eyes and its beak was open in a silent caw. It was carrying something in its claws.

She took all of this in in about three seconds because then she turned around and began pushing her way toward the door.

At the ladder-like pile of boxes, she stopped. She had something else to do, didn't she? She had to climb sideways over the boxes, so she should be sure that she was finished in this room because it would be a real pain to come back.

And she wasn't finished, because she hadn't found the armadillo. Had she even looked for it?

No, she'd been looking in the closet and then...

...then she'd turned around and walked away in a hurry.

Now why did I do that? wondered Rosa.

She went back to the closet, looked at the box with the crow, and found herself back at the pile of boxes again. She had to go do...something...else...didn't she?

No, I don't. I have absolutely nothing else to do, and that's why I'm here. Because I'm bored. Stop telling me I have to go do something else.

Rosa began to get a suspicion about what was going on, but Uncle Alfonso always said that the third time was the charm. She turned back to the closet, keeping her eyes fastened on the ceiling.

When she was firmly in front of the closet shelves, she lowered her gaze slowly.

Top shelf, hat-boxes, nothing.

Next shelf, Coronation calendar and a couple of bags of yarn, nothing.

Middle shelf...

Rosa's feet turned her around and her brain tried to tell her that she had something else to do somewhere else.

"It's an illumination!" said Rosa aloud.

You didn't grow up in a studio full of illumination painters without learning to recognize when a magic charm was actually working on *you*. She didn't recognize the crow and she couldn't look at it long enough to make out what was in its claws, but it was undoubtedly an illumination.

Now that's interesting.

An illumination that could make people go away like that wasn't completely unheard of. Aunt Nadia made illuminations to keep burglars away, sometimes, although they were expensive. They only kept casual burglars from deciding the house looked promising, though; they wouldn't stop someone who was already determined to rob you.

To last this long, and to actually turn somebody around and send them off, instead of just making the box look boring or moldy or covered in spiders...*that* was a powerful illumination.

Why would somebody put an illumination like that on a box? thought Rosa, then immediately answered herself—*To protect something inside it.*

Something valuable.

It could be gold. Jewels. Piles of money. Or something expensive we could sell.

Rosa considered for a few minutes. Then she took out a pen—she always carried a pen in her pocket, because you could be struck by a really good idea for a painting *anywhere* and you had to write it down *at once* or it might be lost forever, and even though all her good ideas seemed to be radish-related, it was still a good habit for an artist to have—and she wrote on her left hand, "crow box in basement."

Then she climbed over the pile of boxes and into the main room.

There was always a way around magic, but sometimes you had to come at it sideways.

One good thing, Rosa knew, as she climbed the stairs up, she was most definitely *not* bored.

SIX

Night
Garlic Day
Messidor, the Month of Harvest

WHEN SHE GOT into the studio, Rosa went at once to the *Iconographer's Concordance*, that other great book, and set a hand on the cover.

The Concordance was the opposite of the Codex. Instead of containing lists of charms, it contained lists of subjects, and would tell you what each one did if you painted it in an illumination.

For example, if you had a painting of a blue-eyed cat, (which you will remember wards away mice) you could look up *cat* and read:

Cat

> *with blue eyes*
> wards away mice
> *with wings*
> brings friendship
> *cat-headed man*
> helps find squirrel nests (best in lockets)

And it would go on for pages and pages like this, every possible variation of cat paintings that did *anything* if you made an illumination of them. Many paintings were so obscure or so useless that there was really no practical reason for them. For example, if you painted a white cat riding on the back of a moose, it would keep your shoelaces from being eaten by badgers. Nobody bothered painting illuminations like that.

Rosa ran a finger over the heavy leather cover. There was a jellyfish embossed on it, holding paintbrushes in its tentacles.

Now what was I going to look up...?

It had seemed important at the time but Rosa was having a hard time remembering now. *Something from the basement, wasn't it? Was there something else I was supposed to do?*

The leather jellyfish had a ridged texture as she rubbed it. She looked down at the cover and at her hand, and read *"crow box in basement"* in smudgy blue ink.

"Ha! You won't get me that easy, crow!"

Uncle Alfonso glanced up from his painting. "Hmmm?"

"I found a neat box in the basement," said Rosa. "It's got an illumination on it to make you leave it alone, though."

"Interesting," said Uncle Alfonso. "I wonder if they had a reason?"

"I'm going to find out."

He nodded. After a moment, he said, "Any luck on the stuffed armadillo front?"

"Sorry, Uncle Alfonso. I didn't see it."

"Ah, well." He sighed. "In life, we are always seeking after something. Love...fame...glory...stuffed armadillos. It is the human condition." He dabbed more paint onto his brush and went back to work.

Rosa opened the heavy cover and dragged the pages over to the C's.

She found the crow section and her heart sank.

There were a *lot* of crow illuminations.

Most animals had at least one illumination attached. Even the hippopotamus could be painted on nail clippers to prevent hangnails. But crows...crows were popular.

Rosa ran her finger down the Concordance. The list of crows went on for six and a half pages, and the print was very small.

There were some very odd notes in it, too.

For example, one said:

Crow
> with two pupils in each eye
> (BANNED. DETAILS REDACTED.)

It wasn't the only listing like that, either. Crows holding salamanders were also banned and redacted, as were crows with their heads cut off—*yuck,* thought Rosa—and crow-headed men holding horse skulls and crows with flaming arrows for tongues.

And yet many of the entries were perfectly normal. Crows holding leafy branches were an illumination to ward off arthritis and a crow holding a glowing seed in its beak kept you from losing your keys.

"Uncle Alfonso?"

"Yes, Rosalita?"

"What does it mean when an entry in the Concordance says, 'Banned. Details Redacted?'"

Uncle Alfonso paused, and then set down his paintbrush. He cleaned his glasses very deliberately on his apron and set them back on his nose. "Well," he said. "Well. It means that painting *that* illumination is forbidden."

"Why would it be forbidden?" asked Rosa.

"Because it does something wicked," said Uncle Alfonso. "It could bring sickness or misfortune or anger. It could bring death." He paused, studying her face. "Creating magic paintings is a responsibility, not just a gift, Rosalita. There are people who will paint unkind paintings and not care who they hurt with it."

Rosa had never heard of bad illumination painters before. It was a fascinating thought. She rubbed her thumb over the word *crow* on her hand, smudging the ink further.

"You never told me about unkind painters before," she said.

Uncle Alfonso shrugged. "There are a great many bad things in the world," he said, "but there is no point in dwelling on them. And there are very *few* makers of such illuminations."

"Have you ever met one?"

"Once," said Uncle Alfonso. "And I do not propose to tell

you about it, Rosalita. It was a long time ago and I was young and foolish."

Rosa scowled horribly, but he wasn't looking at her. Even though she was dying to know about the evil illumination maker, she asked a different question instead.

"What would happen if you painted one of the bad illuminations? By accident?"

"It's rare," said Uncle Alfonso. "We are always very careful when we paint new illuminations. If we're worried, we check the Concordance. But yes, sometimes accidents happen, and then we apologize and we give the client a newer and much better illumination to replace it." He smiled briefly. "Your Cousin Sergio once tried to make a very fancy illumination for a restaurant, of a bird nesting. It was supposed to keep food from spoiling. But he got so carried away painting the branches of the tree that he wove them together into knotwork, and it turns out that knotwork olive branches form an illumination that makes everything in the kitchen taste of sardines. The cook was very upset and we had to sand the painting down and paint another one."

Rosa giggled. "He didn't check for that?"

"Well, it had never come up before. I don't think anyone had any idea." He picked up his paintbrush again. "Very bad illuminations tend to be very *specific* illuminations. If someone wants to do a bad thing, they must be very precise. If you keep the details secret, it's unlikely that someone would stumble on it casually."

Rosa considered this. None of the listings under *crow* said "keep people away" or "make people go do something else." But it was possible that one of the banned illuminations *would* have said that, if the details weren't redacted.

I shall have to look at the box more closely, and see exactly what the crow looks like. Then I'll know what to look for in the book.

But how could she do that when the box kept driving her away?

She closed the Concordance and stared at the jellyfish, thinking.

Even when Grandmama called "Dinner!" and the whole family piled out of their studios and into the kitchen, Rosa did not stop thinking. The answer would come to her, she was sure of it. She just had to keep picking at it.

SEVEN

Morning
Wheat Day
Messidor, the Month of Harvest

WHILE SHE WAS WAITING for the answer to come to her, Rosa set out to make herself useful, and perhaps find a way to restore the Mandolini fortunes.

This was more difficult than she expected.

For one thing, useful things were often not very interesting. Grandmama felt it would be quite useful for Rosa to do the dishes. Rosa did not feel that this was a good use of her talents.

She tried elsewhere. "Uncle Marco? Do you have anything useful I could do?"

"Help me find Walter!" he suggested. "He's wandered off again."

Rosa let out a sigh that seemed to come from the bottom of her toes.

Uncle Marco was painting a commission for a local nursery, to keep the babies from getting diaper rash. For no reason that anyone knew, the illuminations to prevent rash were paintings of stag beetles, which are enormous beetles with large clicky mandibles. They could be any color that you wanted, but they had to have the mandibles.

Nurseries have a lot of babies. Uncle Marco's commission was to paint seventy-three stag beetles on a board twenty feet long. The end of the board stuck out of the bay and people kept having to detour around it.

Uncle Marco preferred to work from life, which meant that every single one of the seventy-three stag beetles was actually based on a single beetle named Walter.

("Why Walter?" Rosa had asked.

"He looks like a Walter," said Uncle Marco.)

He painted them all the colors of the rainbow, red and orange and indigo and violet, but all of them started with Walter. Walter was very well treated, for a beetle, but sometimes he got the urge to go exploring.

"I'll look high and you look low," suggested Uncle Marco.

Uncle Marco had a bad leg and he walked with a cane most of the time, but when he was painting, he sat on a wheeled stool and pushed himself back and forth along the length of the board. He pushed himself along now, checking behind bottles of paint, and Rosa got down on her hands and knees, looking under the table.

Walter was nowhere to be found. "I'll check the other bays," she said.

There were no beetles in Uncle Alfonso's bay, and none in

Grandmama's bedroom. Aunt Nadia was standing in front of her immense painting for the Merchant Council. Each face glowed with angelic light, as if lit from within. Rosa knew that it was a trick done by putting very thin layers of color over bright white paint, but knowing how it was done didn't make it look any less impressive.

The real magic—the power of an illumination that was beginning to come to life—was still faint, but it was growing.

"It's beautiful, Aunt Nadia," Rosa said.

"It's getting there," said Nadia wearily. "So much left to paint..."

She picked up the brush again. Rosa checked in the corners for Walter, but didn't find him.

She went up on the roof, in case Walter had decided to get some fresh air. The air in the city often smelled like—well, like *city*, like dust and horses and people and the strong, murky scent of the canal. But the recent rain had washed the air clean and it smelled like fresh laundry and growing things.

The Studio Mandolini was taller than the three surrounding buildings. Rosa could look down onto the roofs of her neighbors. Everyone had their little rooftop gardens, full of basil and vining tomatoes, all grown in pots with illuminated grape-leaves on them. (Three grape leaves together were a very simple illumination to make plants grow.) Their neighbor on the left kept chickens on the roof, including a very confused rooster who crowed at odd hours. Their neighbor on the right had a laundry line flapping in the breeze.

All the buildings were made of brick, patched with big gray splotches of adobe. Some of the windows were boarded up. There was a spot on the roof where Rosa wasn't supposed to walk because the boards creaked alarmingly. It wasn't the most wealthy neighborhood, but everyone was friendly and pleasant, except for maybe the rooster.

Past the three immediate neighbors, there were much taller buildings. Rosa couldn't see over those. One had a line of rooftop apartments with balconies, and even though they were cheap apartments, the windowboxes spilled over with red geraniums and tumbling orange nasturtiums. Every window had an illumination on it to prevent breakage. If she turned her head right, Rosa could just see the magic out of the corner of her eye, as if the windows were glowing.

Because she was surrounded on all sides by buildings, Rosa sometimes felt like she was in a little valley looking up at mountains. She had never been to the mountains, but she had seen so many paintings of them that she had a fair idea what it must be like.

Serena's rooftop at the Studio Magnifico had a better view. It was taller than the Studio Mandolini and you could see to the market square and one of the canals.

"You can even see the spire of the Great Cathedral, too," Serena had said once. "Look, between those two buildings!"

"I think that's a weathervane," Rosa had said doubtfully.

"No, it isn't. It's the Great Cathedral."

"The Great Cathedral doesn't have a chicken on top of it."

"It's an angel, not a chicken!"

Rosa had decided that she wasn't going to win that one, so she'd changed the subject. "Will you get married in the Great Cathedral?"

"I will!" said Serena. "In a grand procession with people throwing rice. The train of my dress will be twenty feet long and there will be a dozen people to hold it up."

"I'll be the Maid of Honor," said Rosa.

"Of course!" said Serena. "And I'll enter the Cathedral—"

"—Just as a gargoyle descends on the steeple! And swoops off with your husband!"

Serena paused, adjusting her fantasy to accommodate an unexpected gargoyle. "And I shall swoon with horror!" She put the back of her hand to her forehead and staggered backward dramatically (though away from the railing around the roof.)

"Noooo!" cried Rosa. "I shall save you! Where is my sword?"

"I may die of grief!"

"Then I will avenge you!"

Rosa stood on the rooftop and heaved a sigh at the memory. It had been a good game. But she wasn't talking to Serena after she'd been so mean.

"I still think it was a weathervane," she said, trying to cheer herself up. It worked a little, but not as much as she'd hoped.

Despite the view, Walter was nowhere to be seen. Rosa came down the stairs, checking each step for beetles.

At last she wandered into Cousin Sergio's studio and found him painting a mermaid on a door.

"Prevents flooding!" he said, painting scales. It was wonderful to watch. The mermaid's tail was flat green and Sergio had a brush with a lighter shade of green paint on it. He made quick little flicks of the brush and each little flick became a scale and suddenly the flat green paint looked alive, as if the mermaid might dive off the door and into the sea.

Rosa could feel the magic radiating off the painting. It felt like a warm mist against her skin. Cousin Sergio was odd and abrupt and he was always losing things, but he was a great painter. Every scale made the painting more powerful. When he was done, you could pour a hundred of gallons of water outside that door and the inside wouldn't even get damp.

Her radishes didn't have the warm, misty feel of a working illumination, but sometimes there was a strange, here-and-there heat to them, as if she was standing in a breeze that swirled and eddied and occasionally brought a touch of warmth with it. Rosa wasn't sure what to make of that. She hoped that it meant she would be an illuminator someday, when she got older, or got the trick of it, or something. She tried not to think that maybe the radishes were the best she'd ever be able to do.

There was no sound in the studio for a minute but the soft flick of the brush as Sergio highlighted scale after scale and the magic grew and grew.

"She's got awfully pointy teeth," said Rosa, a bit doubtfully.

"Eats sailors! Not nice!"

"Oh," said Rosa. "Like the Sirens in Ulysses—"

And then she had it.

Ulysses, when he wanted to listen to the Sirens, had tied himself to the mast to keep from going to them. Rosa needed to look at the box, but she had to keep herself from going *away*. "Thanks, Sergio!" she cried, and stood on her tiptoes and kissed him on the cheek.

He looked vaguely surprised. "Welcome!"

Rosa ran off in pursuit of twine. (Rope would have been better, but grown-ups tend to ask rather strange questions when you demand to know if there is any rope suitable for tying yourself up with.)

Eventually she found some. Grandmama had bunches of herbs hung up and tied with twine, and both the ball of twine and the big scissors to cut it were in a drawer in the kitchen. Rosa snipped off several generous lengths and stuffed them in her pocket along with the scissors, and went back downstairs to deal with the crow.

She slid and slithered through the stacks to the closet with the crow box. Once she was there, she tied the twine around her wrist, several times, although she was careful not to tie it too tight, because she didn't want to cut off the circulation and have her hand turn black and fall off. (That would have been *very* interesting and not at all boring, but she used her hands a lot and would have found it very inconvenient.)

Rosa tied the other end of the twine to the doorknob on the outside of the closet, careful not to look inside. She couldn't keep her eyes closed and tie the knots at the same time, but she kept one eye closed and her face turned away.

When she had tied herself quite firmly to the doorknob—and had yanked several times and not broken the twine—she took a deep breath and turned to face the crow box.

Let's see, middle shelf...

Her eyes locked on the painted eyes of the crow. She turned immediately away, marching toward the door, and was brought up short by the twine.

Why am I tied to—oh, right...

"Sneaky crow," she said aloud. "Sneaky, sneaky crow. But I'm even sneakier."

She rummaged around for one of the bolts of lace. Her eyes skipped over the crow box twice and the twine jerked her back to reality both times.

Rosa grinned. She was winning.

With the big kitchen scissors, she hacked off a long length of yellow lace. It was not the best material, but it was better than nothing.

She squeezed her eyes shut and began to feel her way down the shelves.

Her fingers crossed wood, old calendars, crumpled fabric... and *there*. It could only be the crow box. It was wood with a complicated sort of latch on it. Rosa could feel the small raised lines of brush strokes.

"Got you," she whispered, and began wrapping lace around the box.

It was surprisingly difficult to do with her eyes closed. Having one wrist tied to the door didn't help. She opened her eyes a crack, spun around, walked toward the door with the strong conviction that the stuffed armadillo was somewhere outside the room, came up short, and grumbled. Apparently she hadn't wrapped it nearly enough.

It took her twenty minutes and she brutalized the bolt of lace in the process. She had to wrap the box four or five times so that it was impossible to make out the pattern through the lace-work. Her wrist was covered in narrow red lines where she yanked on the twine while trying to walk away.

Finally, when she was thoroughly frustrated and thoroughly determined to beat the crow box or die trying, she looked down...and nothing happened.

The box sat on the shelf, a misshapen lump of wrapped and wadded lace. One corner stuck out, but apparently that corner did not have enough of the illumination visible to drive her away.

Rosa blew out her breath through her long black bangs.

"*Well*, then," she said.

She cut the twine holding her to the door and picked up the box.

It wasn't particularly heavy. Probably not stacks of gold,

then. But when she tilted it, she felt something shifting inside, so it wasn't empty.

She cradled it to her chest. She felt a little weird, thinking that the crow was wedged right up against her, glaring through the lace into her lungs and her heart, but it couldn't do anything.

"If you were the sort of illumination that killed people, I'd be dead already," said Rosa. "And who would have put you in the basement, anyway?"

She hefted the box and made her way out through the stacks.

She was most of the way across the studio floor when she spotted Walter trundling determinedly along. She tucked the box under her arm and grabbed him by the shell. His legs kicked and he waved his mandibles in the air, but he was basically a good-natured beetle.

Uncle Marco was overjoyed. "Walter! Why do you wander off, my interesting little friend? I can't do this without you." He held out his hands and Rosa dropped the beetle into them, and left artist and model alone.

She took the box to her bay of the studio and set it down on the bed. She had to think carefully about what to do next.

If I see the crow, it makes me walk away. So if I'm going to open the box, I need to make sure I don't see it.

She tied her wrist to the bedpost with a long piece of twine and stared fixedly at one of her fanged radishes.

She could just close her eyes...but if she opened them on accident, she'd waste a lot of time going back and forth.

"What I need is a blindfold!" said Rosa out loud.

She would have preferred an elegant silk blindfold, something that looked very impressive and sinister. Unfortunately she didn't have anything like that.

She opened her sock drawer and scowled. Rosa had very small feet and the socks were all very short. She would have had to tie three or four together to make a decent blindfold.

On the other side of the drawer, though...

Rosa sighed.

They were clean and they were the right size and she wanted to get into the box *right now,* and that was how she ended up kneeling on the bed with a pair of underwear on her head. She could feel her hair sticking up through the leg holes. *I hope nobody comes in and sees this.*

Still, she had more important things to worry about. Rosa began carefully unwrapping the lace around the box.

She had barely gotten two turns done when Grandmama said "Rosa? Is that *underwear* on your head?"

"No!" said Rosa, snatching it off. "Or—um—yes, but—"

Her grandmother and her uncle were standing in the doorway.

"Why are you...no." Grandmama held up a hand. "I don't want to know. I don't ask Sergio when I come in and he's standing on his head with his eyes closed—"

"Helps me think!" shouted Cousin Sergio, who was headed for the kitchen. "Improves blood flow!"

Uncle Alfonso did not comment, but his lips did twitch just a little. Instead he said, to Rosa, "Would you like to come with me? They are fitting together the great illumination at the sewer, and your grandmother and I are going to watch."

"Yes!" said Rosa, jumping up.

The twine caught her wrist and pulled her back down.

Grandmama covered her face with her hands. "I will not

ask," she said, to no one in particular. "If you are in a family of artists, you learn not to ask. So I will not ask."

Rosa hurriedly cut herself free with the scissors and shoved her feet into her shoes. "Coming, Uncle!"

The crow box was important. But the great illumination that Uncle Alfonso had been part of was the most important work that the city had seen in a hundred years.

EIGHT

Afternoon
Wheat Day
Messidor, the Month of Harvest

IF YOU WERE GOING to make a list of the most glamorous
places on earth, sewers would be unlikely to make the cut.

True, there are some that run through ancient, buried cities
and some that are lined with the bones of unfortunate armies
and some that enter the mouth of a live sea serpent and run out
again through the other end—well, only one of those, to be
precise, located in the ancient and terrible city of Thran, and
tourists do not go to Thran except in small pieces intended for
consumption by the priesthood—but the majority of sewers are
really quite boring.

The sewer in Rosa's city was not one of the exciting ones.

Fortunately, they did not actually have to go down into it. Instead, Uncle Alfonso and Rosa and Rosa's grandmother walked through the tangled streets to the great canal that ran in a slithery half-circle around and through the city.

There were many bridges across the canal, but the bridge they walked to was very wide and had a squat stone building built directly into the surface of the water. A set of stone steps ran down to the water-building's door.

You could smell the canals long before you got to them. They smelled like dead fish and rotten garbage and nobody drank the water. You got water from the well or piped into the house, but you would never, ever drink from the canal itself. The sewers in the city hadn't been dug very deep, and every time it rained they overflowed into the canal. In practice, that meant that if you flushed the toilet during a rainstorm, whatever you flushed went floating by in the canal ten minutes later. It was...unpleasant. The canal was connected on one end to the lake, and once upon a time, the other end had connected to farmer's fields, but eventually the water got so unpleasant that the farmers didn't want it, so it just sat in the canal and stank and occasionally backed up into people's basements.

The Dynast, who ruled the city, aimed to change that, and that was where the city illuminators came in.

Uncle Alfonso knocked on the door of the building and a little man in a hat opened it. He wore a paper mask over the lower half of his face. He tipped his hat to Grandmama, smiled in a vague way at Rosa, and ushered them inside. "Come on," he said. "We're almost ready to start."

They followed the little man into the building. The smell was appallingly bad, even worse than it was outside. Grandmama made a noise and put her hand over her mouth.

"I know," said the little man, "believe me, I know! Put these on, it helps."

He handed them little paper masks. Uncle Alfonso helped tie Rosa's. The mask covered the wearer's nose and mouth, and the paper had been soaked in perfume, so it smelled very strongly of lavender and lemon.

They followed the little man through another door and down a hallway which opened onto an enormous room. A group of illuminators stood there, all wearing paper masks. Rosa recognized Serena's brother by his eyes, and Serena's father by his lack of hair.

They waved to the Mandolinis, and Uncle Alfonso lifted a hand to wave back. Rosa was glad that Serena wasn't there. It would have been very awkward.

It also meant that *she* got to see a great illumination come to life, and Serena didn't. Rosa found this a cheering thought. When they were speaking again—if they were ever speaking again—she was going to tell Serena all about it.

The floor of the enormous room dropped away in front of them, going way down into the ground. There was a railing around it so that people didn't fall in. The Mandolinis went right up to the railing and looked over, and Rosa said, "Ewwww."

On the far wall, there was a gigantic sewer grate. Flowing out of it, dropping into the canal below, was the nastiest, ickiest, grimiest water that Rosa had ever seen.

You could hardly call it water. It didn't trickle, it *oozed*. It was the color of dark coffee and it was thick and sludgy. Green scum hung from the bottom of the grate in slimy ropes.

"That's the sewer outlet," said Serena's brother, leaning against the railing next to Rosa. "Isn't it disgusting?"

Rosa nodded.

"When it rains, it doesn't just dribble out like that. It shoots out like a fire hose." He shuddered theatrically, and Rosa did too.

Rosa tried to imagine that disgusting brown water shooting out like a fire hose and backed away from the edge.

Serena's brother laughed. "They're going to let more water out—oh, look! We're starting!"

Around the rim of the sewer grate, in a circle twenty feet across, were six immense curved tiles. Five had been slotted into place, and only the gap at the top was empty. The tiles were the size of tables, and each one was painted carefully with illuminations.

"Which one's yours?" asked Serena's brother.

"The top right," said Uncle Alfonso. "Which one is Studio Magnifico's?"

"The bottom two," said Serena's brother.

"Fine work," said Uncle Alfonso easily, while Rosa thought *Two! They got to do two tiles?*

"What little you can see of it from here!" said Serena's brother, laughing. "They had to glaze those two twice over, since they'll take a pounding."

Uncle Alfonso had worked on his tile every day for over a month. Everything had to be done with the special glazes that the Dynast's men had supplied, and then the tile had been taken and fired in a kiln and glazed again so that the water wouldn't wear it away. The glazes had been thick and turned heavy as mud if you left them for long, so Rosa had spent hours stirring the pots while her uncle worked.

But why did the Studio Magnifico get to paint two tiles, and we only got to paint one?

While she was thinking these gloomy thoughts, two men went along the walkways, and began hauling on ropes. Grandmama pointed, and Rosa looked up and saw the last and largest tile being lowered from the ceiling.

"Who did that one?" asked Uncle Alfonso.

"Studio Lasrina, I think," said Serena's brother. "The one that keeps all the barky little dogs." He grinned. "I guess all the dog hair burns off when they fire the tile in the kiln."

The tile was lowered until it was nearly in front of the gap in the circle. Uncle Alfonso reached out and took Rosa's hand, and she realized that he was nervous.

Why would he be nervous? He's been an illuminator for years and years, I know he did it right!

"Please let this work," muttered Serena's brother, almost to himself. "And if it doesn't work, let it be someone else's fault and not mine..."

Uncle Alfonso laughed. "From your lips to the ears of the saints!"

The last tile slotted into place.

For a moment nothing happened, and then Rosa began to feel...something.

At first she thought that the smell really was making her dizzy, but it was clear that everyone else felt it too. A wind seemed to blow from nowhere. The warm feeling of an illumination coming to life began to fill the air, but it was stronger than anything Rosa had ever felt.

"Five studios..." murmured the little man in the hat. "Two years to get the design right..." He wrung his hands together. "If it works, the illuminations will keep all that nasty stuff in the sewer, and only let pure water through...*if* it works..."

"If it works," said Uncle Alfonso, "the canals will be clean.

People will be able to drink from them. No more walking blocks to a well, if there isn't a pipe."

He squeezed Rosa's hand.

Rosa tried to picture it. They had piped water at home, but in the poor parts of the city, people still had to use wells and pumps. Grandmama had said that when she was young, before the pipes had been installed, she had to spend hours every day fetching enough water to cook and bathe and clean brushes with. Rosa could hardly imagine how much *work* that must have been.

"And no more smell!" said Serena's brother.

"Can illuminations *do* that?" asked Rosa. There was a canal less than a block away, and in summer you could smell it even indoors. They burned sweet candles by the armload to purify the air.

The notion that a simple painting, even a magical one, could clean the horrible sludge coming out of the grate boggled the mind.

"Look!" said Grandmama.

The mortar between the tiles, previously invisible, began to glow.

Golden light bathed their faces. Serena's brother put up a hand to shield his eyes.

The wind intensified. Even through the mask, Rosa could smell it. It smelled of clean pine and cedar, and it swirled around them, tugging at her hair and the paper mask, cutting through the scent of waste and lavender.

The pipe behind the grate began to rumble.

"They're releasing the water now," said the little man in the hat. He sounded as if he were watching an execution. "Oh please, please, Saint Anthony, please..."

With a roar, water poured through the pipe and struck the grate. Rosa jumped back. The sound of the water hitting the metal was like an immense fist striking a board. The whole room shuddered with the impact.

The golden light from between the tiles blazed up to meet it. It was so bright that Rosa couldn't even see what was happening at first—and then the light ran down the metal of the grate, running over the iron bars like golden syrup, until a spiderweb of light covered the opening.

For a moment, Rosa saw what looked like a dark serpent, thirty yards long, thrashing inside the pipe, ramming against the web of light, as all the filth in the sewer struck the illumination...and was thrown back.

Water poured out of the grate, reflecting a hundred sparks of the golden light, and it was as clean and clear as the water that came out of the pipes in the studio. The horrible sludge was gone.

One of the men on the walkway put out a cup on a long pole and filled it with the clear water. He passed his hands over it, carefully—"Water-witch," murmured Serena's brother—and then nodded.

He brought the cup back with him, to the little man in the hat.

"It's clean, sir," he said.

Rosa could actually see the little man's hands shaking as he looked into the cup.

He lifted it to his lips and took a drink. He closed his eyes.

And nodded.

"It worked," the man whispered. "Saints have mercy on us. It worked."

NINE

"It will take a bit for the canals to be clean," said Uncle Alfonso, as they made their way home. "They're going to drain them, a little at a time, into the sewer so that the water can pass through the illumination. And someone will have to muck out the sewer itself, which is a whole different set of problems. But now we'll have clean water everywhere in the city, not just for the people who can afford wells and good pipes."

Rosa nodded. She was tired and her head ached from the remembered smell of lavender, but she was proud of her uncle and what he had helped to do.

He smiled down at her. "Not very impressive looking, eh, Rosalita? All that work just to clean some gunk out of water."

"It *was* impressive," said Rosa, thinking of the thing like a serpent made of grime, thrashing against the web of magic. "And it'll help a lot of people."

He squeezed her shoulder, and she knew that she'd pleased him. "It will. That's what the best illuminations do. Most of them are little tiny things, like keeping the milk from going bad, or keeping the mice out of the pantry, but they make people's lives a little better. That's the best that any of us can hope for."

He straightened. "Now let's go get something to celebrate."

"We can't afford it," said Grandmama sadly.

"We can afford a lemon ice," said Uncle Alfonso firmly. "They are a fine dessert and they cost very little."

"It's the middle of the day," said Grandmama, sounding amused.

"Then if we die before dinner, at least we will have had dessert," said Uncle Alfonso grandly, and all three of them laughed.

When they had ices in hand and were walking back to the studio, Rosa finally asked the question that was on her mind. "Why did the Studio Magnifico get two tiles, and we only got one?"

"Because they could get two of them done," said Uncle Alfonso, "and we could not."

"Because there's more of them?"

"Mmm. Yes, but not just that." Uncle Alfonso tilted his hand back and forth, nearly upsetting his ice. "Their studio works together on pieces. Three or four of them could work on each tile. We don't do that."

"Why not?"

"Because," said Grandmama dryly, "if you ask two Mandolinis how to do something, you will get five different answers."

Rosa's uncle grinned. "We do not work so well together, it is true. Not when it comes to magic. We each have our own ideas how things should be done. If we try to work together, we get under each other's feet. So we must each do our own."

"But why couldn't you have done two? If you had time?"

"Do you remember when I told you that a painting takes a little bit of your heart?" Uncle Alfonso asked. Rosa nodded. "Well, you are young and strong and your heart grows by leaps and bounds. But when you get older, it takes longer. Such a large illumination takes a large piece of your heart, and it does not grow back so easily. If you do too many, too quickly, you will find yourself with only a tired sliver left, and then you're in trouble."

"Will you *die?*" whispered Rosa, horrified.

Grandmama snorted. "No," she said, "but you will lie around and mope and pick at your food for days, until your family is sick to death of it."

"You must feed your heart," said Uncle Alfonso. "With beautiful things and places you have never seen and books that bring you joy. Then your heart will grow back and you can paint again. But I knew, you see, that I could not do two of those tiles. It would take too much out of me, at my age."

Rosa heaved a sigh. "I wish I could make illuminations."

"You will, Rosalita. I have faith." He thumped his chest with his fist. "You are one of the Mandolinis, after all, and we are known for the greatness of our hearts."

WHEN THEY REACHED the studio at last, only slightly slowed by the stop for lemon ice, Rosa hurried back to her room.

I don't think I can do anything like those huge sewer illuminations, but maybe I can figure out what's in this box. Maybe it'll be something valuable. The box was too light to have gold coins, but there might be gems.

She dragged her wooden privacy screen across the entry-way. *I should have done that last time. Then Grandmama wouldn't have seen me with underwear on my head.*

The box was still there. She put her makeshift blindfold back over her head, sat down, and began unwrapping it.

When she was down to bare wood, she brushed her fingers across it. She could feel the slightly raised texture of brush strokes. *That must be the crow.* She felt for the latch.

It felt complicated. She wasn't sure how much of that was because she was blindfolded and couldn't actually see it. There was no keyhole, but there were two little bars on either side and a little square bit and two round pegs...

Rosa frowned. She had no idea what she was supposed to do to open the lock.

She squeezed one side and then the other. She tried twisting the square bit and pulling on the pegs. Nothing happened.

Or...almost nothing.

Very faintly, under her fingers, she felt a tremor.

With renewed interest, she wiggled the lock. She tried grabbing both bars and pushing.

The box trembled again. It felt less like a mechanism and more like something alive.

"Almost..." Rosa muttered.

The box gave a sudden violent shudder. Rosa jerked back, startled. She was still holding the bars and when she jumped, she pulled them outward.

The lock clicked open.

The box lid fell backward. Something leapt over Rosa's hand and ran up her arm. It felt like insect feet. It felt *nasty*. Rosa yelped.

She shook her arm violently and whatever-it-was went flying. She heard a rustle as it ran out of the studio, but it was gone before she could even reach her hand up to her blindfold.

A weight landed on her shoulder.

"Rawwwk!" said a frantic, gravelly voice next to her ear. "Close the box, quick!"

Rosa hurried to obey the voice. She slammed the lid closed, holding her breath.

If she was hoping that this would appease the voice, she was disappointed. On her shoulder, something moved and flapped.

"*Rawwk!* You've let the Scarling out! Why would you *do* such a thing? Who *are* you? And why are you wearing underwear on your head?"

TEN

Evening
Wheat Day
Messidor, the Month of Harvest

ROSA TRIED to pull the underwear off her head, but she used the hand still tied to the bedpost, so her wrist jerked to a halt. She had to fumble with the other hand before she got it off.

There was a crow on her shoulder.

"Rawwk!" said the crow. "That's better, but what were you thinking?"

"I needed a blindfold," said Rosa weakly. What she was thinking was, *Oh my goodness, is the crow actually talking?*

She'd read stories about talking animals, of course, but they were mostly mythological. She hadn't expected it to happen in real life.

The crow considered this. "Rrrrr. I suppose that would work."

From outside, Rosa heard Aunt Nadia say "Rosa, darling? Are you all right? I heard you yelling..."

"Ack!" said the crow, in a much quieter voice. He hopped down onto Rosa's bed, and then to the floor, scuttling under it. "Don't tell anyone I'm here!"

"I'm fine, Aunt Nadia," said Rosa hurriedly, as her aunt appeared at the opening of the bay. "Just thought I saw a mouse."

"A mouse?" Nadia frowned. "We'll have to do the illuminations up again. Unless you've been painting their eyes different colors again."

"No!" said Rosa hotly. Sometimes grown-ups never let you forget *anything*. "That was years ago!"

"All right," said Nadia.

Rosa waited until her aunt had left before looking at the box. The painted crow had vanished. It was only a background of leaves and twining twigs, and a pair of dragonflies with their wings crossed over each other.

Whatever magic compulsion it had held was gone.

Does that mean the crow is the crow from the box?

Rosa had heard stories of powerful illuminations before, of course. There were legends about illuminations that could talk. It was even said that long ago a warlord had kept a roll of cloth with an army painted on it, and when he shook the cloth out, the army would come to life and battle his enemies.

But those were all legends, like Ulysses and the sirens. She had never heard of such a thing happening in real life, and certainly not in the city. The Studio Mandolini were the best illuminators around—no matter what Serena said!—and none of them could have made an illumination come to life. An army of illuminations was no more real than an army made of dragon's teeth.

She flopped over on the bed and hung her head over the edge.

"Rawk," said the crow, but quietly. He turned his head and one bright eye caught the light. "Is she gone?"

"Yes," whispered Rosa. "But why don't you want her to see you?"

"Too many people," said the crow. "The more people who know about the Scarling, the harder it is to keep it quiet. If word gets out, people will panic, or they'll want it for themselves." He narrowed his eyes suspiciously. "Are *you* after it?"

"What's a Scarling?" asked Rosa.

The crow blinked. It was hard to tell with a bird, but she thought he might be astonished. "It's the *Scarling*," he said. "You really don't know?"

"No!"

"Rawk! No wonder you were so eager to let it out!"

Rosa flushed. "I didn't mean to let anything out! The box was interesting, that's all."

The crow put his head under his wing and groaned.

"I told him," he muttered. "I told him and told him. 'Make a magical box, people are going to want to know what's in it!' I said, 'You might as well put a sign on it saying PLEASE OPEN.' But he didn't listen. He never listens. Always thinks he knows best."

"Who are you talking about?" asked Rosa.

The crow moved his wing. "Don't you know? My master, Tybalt Mandolini."

He said it as if it were an important name, the sort of name that Rosa would have read about at the parish school, instead of someone (presumably a relative) that Rosa had never heard of.

"Um," said Rosa. She knew her parents' names, although they were dead, and her aunts and uncles and cousins, but she had never heard of a single one named Tybalt. "Do you mean Tiberius?" She had a third cousin named Tiberius, although he wasn't technically a Mandolini, and Grandmama said that she didn't know what his mother was thinking, saddling him with a name like that.

"I most certainly do *not* mean Tiberius," said the crow. "My master's name is Tybalt." He gave her another suspicious look. "Where did you find the box?"

"It was just sitting in the basement."

The crow made a dry *harrumph* sound. "A likely story. What day is it?"

"Wheat Day."

"Wheat *what?*"

"Wheat Day. In the month of Messidor."

The crow looked at her as if she'd grown another head. "You named a day after *wheat?* What *year* is it?"

Rosa had liked stories about talking animals when she was younger. She'd made up a few herself. None of them had involved the animals interrogating her about the date.

"It's 63," said Rosa.

The crow turned its head back and forth several times, to stare at her out of each eye in turn. Rosa thought he was astonished. "What, 1663?"

"No," said Rosa. "Just 63."

"It can't be," said the crow. "I went onto the box in 1644. It can't be 63. It'd be a thousand years earlier, plus change. Time doesn't work like that. You go forwards not back."

Rosa wracked her memory. Something about calendars and a switch and a revolution...there had been a test on it at the school, but it had been ages ago. Still, the numbers made her think of something she'd seen, something to do with art...

"The painting in Grandmama's bedroom!" she said. "It's signed down in the corner, and dated, and it's a long number like that."

"Take me to see it," said the crow. "I want to get to the bottom of this."

This was easier said than done. Rosa had to bundle the crow up in her jacket because he was determined that no one see him. She felt silly carrying her jacket around indoors, particularly since it was so warm out, but her family were all busy painting and nobody looked at her twice. Grandmama herself was out at the market picking up groceries for dinner.

She smuggled the crow into the bay where her grandmother slept and then unwrapped the jacket. His feathered head popped up, looking rumpled. "Awk! I thought you were going to carry me, not smother me!"

Rosa was starting to think that the crow was extremely difficult to please.

"It's over here," she said, and brought the crow to the big oil painting that dominated one wall of the bay.

The painting was a landscape of the countryside outside of the city. The hills were crossed with vineyards and in the foreground, a tiny figure and a donkey made their way down a dusty road.

"Sentimental tripe," said the crow.

"I like it," said Rosa, stung. When she had slept on the couch in the bay, she had looked at the painting while she fell asleep and dreamed about walking along that road to the distant blue hills.

The crow glanced at her. "Well," he said grudgingly, "I suppose it's pretty good technique. Where's the signature?"

He hopped up on an end table and peered at the bottom right corner of the painting.

The signature was long and swoopy and impossible to read. (Rosa had tried.) But the date was very clear.

"1788...?" said the crow in a very small voice.

"There," said Rosa. "See? That's an old date. Before they changed the calendar after the revolution." She was pleased to have remembered this much.

"Revolution?" said the crow blankly.

"Well, it wasn't here," said Rosa. "It was in another country. But they changed the calendar because they said the old one was superstitious and full of the names of bad people. And then some of the other countries had revolutions and started using the calendar too and then it was just easier to use that one because it was really confusing if we were the only ones who didn't."

"Oh," said the crow weakly. "Was it?"

"Well, yes. If you said that you would have a painting finished by Thermidor and nobody knew when that was, they might show up a month early asking where their painting was."

The crow's beak gaped open in distress.

"Anyway, it's interesting," said Rosa. "I mean, I was born on Chive Day! And chives have pink flowers that you can eat and they taste sort of garlicky. Cousin Sergio did a drawing of chives for me on my birthday. They didn't used to have names for days like that. Who'd want to be born on just a number?"

The crow, perhaps overwhelmed by this revelation, gazed at her in amazement.

After a moment, he said "What year was the revolution, then?"

"Year one?" said Rosa.

"No, in the old calendar," said the crow.

Rosa hadn't done very well on that test. "Um. Seventeen ninety...something. I think. Sorry. I don't know exactly."

The crow stuck his head under his wing.

Rosa blinked.

"Two hundred years!" said the crow, somewhat muffled by feathers. "It's been over two hundred years! By all the saints who look kindly on corvids, how could he *do* this to me?"

"Two hundred years since what?" asked Rosa.

"Since Tybalt put me on the box! Awk!"

He trailed off into sad little chirps. Rosa reached out hesitantly and patted his wing. His feathers were warm and dry and rather stiff. "Um? Are you okay, crow?"

"Rrrrrkkkrr...."

"I don't know what that means, crow."

The wing heaved as the crow sighed. He poked his head back out. "My name's not Crow," he said. "It's Payne."

"Pain?" said Rosa. "Like being in pain?" This seemed ominous.

"No," said the crow. "*Payne.* With a Y."

"Oh, like Payne's Gray!" Payne's Gray was a color of paint, a blue so dark it was almost black. Uncle Alfonso said that it was one of the most useful colors for an artist, along with Sepia and Unbleached Titanium. (Some colors of paint have very unusual names. There was even a color called Mummy Brown, and it was best not to ask what it was made of.)

"Yes," said Payne. "Exactly right." He spread his wing out and Rosa could see that it was indeed a deep blue-black. "Hmm. Maybe you're not completely hopeless. What's your name?"

"Rosa Mandolini," said Rosa.

ELEVEN

Evening
Wheat Day
Messidor, the Month of Harvest

THE CROW SNAPPED his beak shut.

He looked at her for a long time, turning his head back and forth again.

"You don't look anything like him," he said finally. "But I suppose it's been two hundred years. And if you're a Mandolini, that would explain why the box would open for you."

He looked up, over the walls of the bay, and then launched himself suddenly into the air. Rosa took a step back.

Everyone's going to see him! she thought, but he dropped down and landed on her shoulder almost immediately.

"This is the old studio," he said. "It *is*. The walls are in the wrong place and it's too big by half, but it's mostly the old studio."

Rosa had nearly exhausted her store of family history at this point, but this one she knew well. "There was a fire," she said. "When I was very small. My parents died."

"I'm sorry," said Payne. Rosa felt his beak against her skin and realized that he was preening her hair. It tickled.

"It's okay," said Rosa. "I don't remember any of it. They had to rebuild, though, and there's still black bricks in the kitchen where it was burnt."

Payne sighed. "I'm being selfish," he said. "Here I am moping just because I've been on a box for two hundred years. Tybalt was supposed to get me back off the box once he found a way to stop the Scarling for good. It was only supposed to take a month or two. Something must have happened to him before he could do that, though. Something bad. And now the Scarling's loose and we need to stop it."

"But what *is* a Scarling?" asked Rosa.

"A rogue illumination," said Payne. "You take a mandrake root and paint the strokes of life on it and if it works, you've got a Scarling. It takes sustenance from other illuminations, and drains their magic dry."

Rosa wasn't quite sure what a mandrake root was. There was a Mandrake Day on the calendar, but it was in spring and she couldn't remember if she'd ever seen a drawing of one. "That sounds bad?" she said.

"It's very bad! It could bring the city to its knees! Imagine if it drained the magic from the illuminations that protect the studio against fire and flood and plague and...and..."

"Mice in the pantry?"

"Ye-e-e-s," said Payne slowly. "Yes. Them too. Not quite the same level of threat as fire and flood, you understand."

He shook his feathers out, which reminded Rosa irresistibly of the way that Aunt Nadia would shake out her coat before she put it on. "I have to think," he said. He began to pace back and forth, bobbing as he walked. "Tybalt gone. Two hundred years! But the Scarling's out—Oh, what do I *do?*"

Rosa heard the kitchen door open, and her grandmother come in. "Take me back to your room," the crow said. "I have to make sure the box is empty. If it is, then it's got the charcoal and we're in real trouble."

So Rosa bundled Payne up again in her coat and snuck back across the studio, her mind a whirl of charcoal and mandrake roots and ancient revolutions.

She got most of the way to her room when the door opened and her grandmother called "Rosa! Come help me with these onions!"

"Just a moment, Grandmama!" Rosa called back. "I have to go," she said to Payne. "I'll be right back, I promise."

"But—"

"Rosa!"

"But I haven't told you—"

She ran to go help her grandmother. Her last sight was of the crow perched on the box, his wings half-spread and his beak open in distress.

HELPING her grandmother chop onions led to helping prepare dinner which led to doing the dishes which meant that Rosa did not get back to her bay until late evening.

She did learn one thing, though. As her grandmother was

dishing out eggplant baked in sauce, Rosa said, "What's mandrake?"

"Ah!" said Uncle Alfonso, smiling. "A wicked plant, Rosalita. Old and fell."

"Rank superstition, darling," said Aunt Nadia.

"Type of root!" barked Sergio. "Not nice!"

"Very interesting plant," said Uncle Marco. He began to sketch on the tablecloth. (Grandmama sighed and rolled her eyes, but didn't stop him.) "People used to think it looked like a little human, because of the way the roots grew."

His sketch did indeed look like a strange little person with long, tapering roots and no head or neck.

"The old story was that if you pulled it, it would scream," said Uncle Alfonso. "And anyone who heard the scream died."

"They'd tie it to a dog's tail," said Uncle Marco, shading in his drawing, "so that the dog would pull it, not a person."

"But what about the poor dog?" asked Rosa. "That doesn't sound very nice for it!"

"Perhaps dogs were immune," said Grandmama.

"Or perhaps in old times, they didn't care as much as they should about dogs," said Uncle Alfonso.

Rosa had to remind herself that the mistreatment of historical dogs was not the important thing at the moment. "What would happen if you put an illumination on one?"

Suddenly the entire family was looking at her. It was a little unsettling. "I wasn't going to," said Rosa hurriedly. "I mean, it's not like I have a mandrake root. I just read about one and I was wondering..."

"Probably nothing," said Aunt Nadia. "It was just an old superstition."

"Maybe..." said Uncle Marco. "Or it might be very interesting indeed..."

"Interesting *how?*" asked Rosa. You could never be sure with Uncle Marco if the things he found interesting would interest a normal person or not.

Her uncle lifted his hands. "Some illuminations change depending on what you paint them on, you know. Canvas and wood and stone are safe enough. Silk is..."

"Pointy!" interrupted Cousin Sergio. "Makes it sharp!" He must have seen that Rosa was puzzled, because he tried to explain. "The magic! On the silk! Feels sharper!"

"Something like that," said Marco. "If you painted the same illumination on silk and on canvas, the silk one wouldn't last as long, but it would be stronger." He smiled. "And the great illumination in the sewer pipe—those were on ceramic so that they would last a very long time and could not be worn away."

"It's not just that," said Aunt Nadia, tapping a nail on the rim of her coffee cup. (Aunt Nadia drank coffee at breakfast, lunch, dinner, and occasionally in the middle of the night when she had trouble sleeping.) "If you painted an illumination so you wouldn't lose your keys, the one on canvas would help you remember. But the one on silk might make you check on your keys every five minutes to make sure you hadn't lost them. Silk is very aggressive like that. *Pointy,* as Sergio says."

"So," said Uncle Marco, "there are many things you could paint an illumination on. People even get them tattooed on themselves. But I've never heard of anyone putting one on a mandrake root. It might simply not work, or it might twist the illumination around in ways we've never seen."

"Best not to try it," said Grandmama firmly, and then she brought out cake and Rosa decided to let the matter drop.

· · ·

AFTER THE DISHES WERE DONE, Rosa dried her hands on a dishtowel and ran for her bedroom.

It was silent. The box still lay open on the floor, but she couldn't see Payne.

"Payne?" she whispered. "Payne, are you here?"

For a moment she heard nothing, and then from the corner, where the bed cast the deepest and darkest shadows, she saw feathers move.

"It doesn't matter," he said mournfully. "We're doomed. Even more doomed than we were before."

"Are we?" asked Rosa.

She was somewhat skeptical of this. Serena had a tendency, when they were playing Great Beauties, to contract a hideous wasting disease or be kidnapped by bandits (sometimes both) and to swoon back across her bed, crying, "We are doomed! *Doomed!*"

The problem then was that Rosa would say, "I'll save us! I kick the bandits in the face!" and then Serena would get upset because once you were doomed, you weren't supposed to get un-doomed so easily.

"The charcoal is gone too," said Payne. "The Scarling took it. I should have checked right away. I was so upset about it being two hundred years, and I didn't think...I'm only a *painted* crow. I'm not quite as clever as the real thing."

Rosa sat down on the bed and stroked his feathers. He felt like a real crow, or at least like the taxidermy one that Uncle Marco used as a model sometimes. (It occurred to her that she should probably not tell Payne about this.) "Start at the beginning," she said, which is what Uncle Alfonso always said when she was upset.

Payne sighed, but turned to face her. "The Scarling has a stick of charcoal," he said. "Like vine charcoal, you know?"

Rosa nodded. Vine charcoal came in thin, wavy little sticks. A burner outside of town burnt vines in his kiln and made them. You could draw with them and they made beautiful smudgy black and gray marks, but they got all over your fingers. Cousin Sergio sketched everything out in vine charcoal instead of pencil and left black smudges on his clothes and the walls and occasionally the toilet paper. Grandmama was forever grumbling about it.

"Right," said Payne. "The Scarling's charcoal is made out of one of its own roots. It's tougher than vine charcoal. It can draw things with it and...well, it's bad."

He hopped over the box. "When Tybalt and I caught it the first time, we had to slam it into the box and we didn't have a chance to get the charcoal away from it so it must still have it and there's no limit to what mischief it can do with it!"

Rosa's eyes were starting to glaze over from all the *its*. "If it's had the charcoal all along, then we're not any *more* doomed," she pointed out. "We're exactly the same amount of doomed as before."

"I suppose," said Payne grudgingly. "But we could have been *less* doomed."

Rosa sighed. "So how do we catch this Scarling, anyway?"

Payne stood on one foot and scraped his claws along his beak, thinking. "It's weak right now. It hasn't had time to regain its strength. If we can catch it and imprison it again before it has time to work mischief, we'll all be far better off."

"All right," said Rosa. "How do we imprison it?"

"We find it," said Payne. "And then we grab it."

"Uh-huh."

"And then..." He leaned in close. "...we stuff it back in the box and close the lid!"

Rosa felt a pang of disappointment. The way Payne had been talking, she had expected something a bit more complicated, possibly involving magic.

"That doesn't sound too tough," she said.

"Don't underestimate the Scarling. It's made of cunning. And wickedness. And...um...wood. Mostly wood. But also wickedness." He snapped his beak. "We should start looking right now. I'll scout overhead. Quietly. And you go around and look for signs of it."

"What does it look like?" asked Rosa, thinking of the mandrake that Uncle Marco had drawn on the tablecloth.

"Like the essence of wickedness!"

"Right, okay, but what does the essence of wickedness *look* like?"

"Like a little brown carrot with legs," said Payne. "And a disagreeable expression."

Rosa sighed again. She'd wanted to do something to help the studio, and instead she was hunting for an evil walking carrot. Maybe Serena had been right, and the Mandolinis *were* weird.

She left the bay and heard a soft wash of feathers behind her as Payne took to the air.

TWELVE

Morning
Velvetleaf Day
Thermidor, the Month of Heat

"Rosa, dear," said Grandmama the next morning over breakfast, "please don't draw on the walls."

Rosa blinked at her over her eggs.

She had been up very late, going from bay to bay, but she hadn't found any sign of the Scarling. She still wasn't entirely sure what she was looking for, but whatever it was, she hadn't seen it.

Payne hadn't come back, either. Eventually she'd gone to bed.

"Do what?" she said.

"Draw on the walls," said Grandmama. "The little doodle

you left in the hallway. I know everybody draws on everything around here, but we have to draw the line somewhere."

"Or not draw the lines, as the case may be," said Aunt Nadia. She never ate any breakfast, just drank cup after cup of black coffee.

"But I didn't," said Rosa. "I don't draw on the walls, you know that."

"Somebody did," said Grandmama. "And I won't have it! The tablecloth, fine. Napkins, fine. I am used to living with artists. But not the walls! Otherwise the studio will look like a public restroom!"

It was true. Grandmama had always been very strict about this. A mural was one thing, that was *art*, but she said that once you started jotting your shopping list down on the wall, they were on the road to Degeneracy. (When she was younger, Rosa had believed that Degeneracy must be a place, apparently with a great deal of graffiti and unmade beds.)

Rosa finished her breakfast, dumped the dishes in the sink, and went into the hallway. She had to look around for the drawing, but she found it at last.

It was about two inches off the floor, just above the baseboard. It was a crude little doodle, two eyes and a scowl with pointy teeth and scribbly lines that might have been hair or spikes or bristles.

"I didn't draw that," said Rosa.

Grandmama sighed. It was the sigh that said she didn't believe you, but didn't want to waste time arguing about it. "Just clean it up, Rosa."

Rosa went back to her room first. "Payne?" she whispered. "Payne, are you here?"

The walls of the bays were only about nine feet high, with

the enormous open ceiling of the studio above them. A dark lump was perched in the shadow where the walls met the brick of the building.

"Payne, is that you?"

Payne ignored her. He seemed to be fixated on something held in his talons.

"Payne?"

"*Look* at it..." breathed the crow.

Rosa dragged her chair over to the wall and climbed up on the seat so that she could get a better look.

"It's a spoon," she said doubtfully.

"It's so *shiny!*" said Payne. He turned the spoon, gazing rapturously at his upside-down reflection in the bowl. "Look how shiny it is!"

Rosa rubbed her forehead. "Did the Scarling drop it or something?"

"What? No! The Scarling doesn't like shiny things. It draws all over them." He clutched the spoon close to his feathers. "We have to protect this one! What if it takes it?"

"Then we'll have to get another spoon," said Rosa. "And anyway—"

"There are *more?!*"

"Sure. A whole drawer full. Where did you get that one?"

"Your aunt had it in her coffee mug. I took it. It's so beautiful."

Rosa thought she might be getting a headache. Maybe it was because she was rolling her eyes so hard. "Look, Payne, this is important! Something's happened."

Payne coughed and tucked the spoon into a nook in the wall. "Right. Important. Tell me."

"There's a drawing in the hall! Grandmama thinks I did it, but I didn't!"

Payne hopped down onto her bed. "Show me."

"Can't you talk to her? If you tell her I didn't do it—"

The crow shook his head violently. "No! The fewer people who know about me, the better!"

"But—"

"No! I'm not talking to anyone! What if they want to put me in a zoo?"

"A zoo? What?"

"I'm a talking crow," said Payne, as if she were being dense. "I am undoubtedly very valuable. If word gets out, I'll end up in a zoo with people staring at me and making me recite epic poetry for their entertainment. And I don't even *like* poetry."

"But—"

"And if they found out I was a living illumination, it would be *much* worse." Payne fluffed up all his feathers and shook like a dog. "They'd want to take me apart and find out how I worked. I'd get scraped and erased down to my bones."

Rosa gritted her teeth. Payne had a point, but she hated having her grandmother thinking that she'd drawn on the walls. It wasn't *fair*.

"You'll have to hide me," said Payne. "Up here with the high ceiling is one thing, but the kitchen is another. I'll never understand why humans like such low ceilings where they eat..."

She smuggled the crow into the hallway. He stuck his head out of a sleeve and studied the drawing. "Scarling," he whispered. "That's its work, all right. I knew it wouldn't leave."

"Why not?"

"Because it hates the Mandolinis," said Payne matter-of-factly. "And it hates me most of all."

Rosa stared down at the crow, her eyes wide.

"It's a long story," he said. (When Aunt Nadia said that, it meant that she had no desire to tell the story, long or not. Rosa wondered if Payne meant it the same way.) "But that's not important now. We can still catch it!"

Rosa had a hard time sharing his enthusiasm, since she was the one who was going to have to clean the wall.

"But—"

"Not in the middle of the hall," said Payne, retreating into her jacket. "Later."

Rosa returned the crow to her bedroom, where he returned to contemplating the shiny spoon, rolled up her sleeves, and filled a bucket with soapy water.

"Something spill?" asked Uncle Alfonso, coming into the kitchen.

"There's a drawing in the hall by the kitchen," said Rosa bitterly, "and Grandmama thinks I did it, but I *didn't!*"

Uncle Alfonso peered at her over his coffee cup. "I believe you, Rosalita," he said, after a long moment. "Do you know who did?"

Rosa stared into the soapy water. Payne was convinced that nobody needed to know about the Scarling...and to be honest, Rosa would have liked to catch it herself, so she didn't have to explain that she'd let a weird little monster loose. She was trying to help the studio, after all, and releasing the Scarling certainly didn't count as helping at *all*.

But what am I going to say? That an evil carrot did it? No one's going to believe that. I hardly believe it myself. She shook her head.

Uncle Alfonso didn't ask her any more questions. He was a good uncle that way. Instead he squeezed her shoulder with his big, paint-stained hand, and left the kitchen.

There might have been a tear or two in the soapy water after that.

Rosa sniffled and wiped her nose. There was no point in crying. She still had to catch the Scarling. More importantly, she had to clean up the mess it had left in the hall.

Why does it hate the Mandolinis? What did we ever do to it?

Did some enemy of Tybalt's make it, two hundred years ago?

That made some sense. It did not, however, get the drawing cleared away.

She picked up the bucket of hot water with both hands and trudged into the hall.

The drawing was gone.

THIRTEEN

ROSA STARED at the blank space for a long time. It had been right there...hadn't it?

She turned and looked down the hall in both directions. There were no drawings anywhere.

Did someone else clean it up? Would Uncle Alfonso have done it? But I only told him a minute ago, and where would he have gotten the soap and water?

She felt a bit lightheaded, as if she was coming down with a fever. *I know I didn't imagine it. Grandmama saw it first.*

Could the Scarling have cleaned it up? But why?

She lugged the bucket back to the kitchen, tipped it out, and rubbed her hands. The handle had left red lines in her palms.

"Payne?" she whispered, entering her bedroom. "Payne, the drawing's gone!"

The crow was standing on her desk, studying the drawings of fanged radishes. "Quite a collection you've got here."

"I like fanged radishes," said Rosa.

"They feel like they want to be illuminations," said Payne thoughtfully. "Except they aren't, quite."

Rosa flopped down on the bed. "I know," she said gloomily. "Uncle Alfonso says that they're art, even if they aren't magic," she said. "But the thing is, they're *almost* magic! I just don't know what they want to be. If I could figure out what they're missing, I'd draw it in and then they'd do...something." She sighed. "I went through the Codex and the Compendium looking. Twice! But the only radishes in the Codex are winged radishes to ward off sickness."

Payne tilted his head and stood on one foot. He reached out with the other and tapped the bottommost radish, tracing the outline with his claw. "Something's missing," he said. "Not wings. It's...oh, I can almost feel it...light or the sun or something..."

Rosa leaned forward.

Payne flexed his claws, not quite creasing the paper. After a moment he shook his head. "Can't figure it out. Sorry."

Rosa realized that she'd been holding her breath and let it out, disappointed. Still, the radishes were an old mystery, and she had other things to worry about. "The Scarling's drawing vanished," she said.

"What?"

"It's gone. I went to clean it up but it's not there."

"Awk! Bad! RAWK!"

He cawed much too loudly for the enclosed space. A babble of voices started up immediately outside the bay.

"What was *that*?"

"Did anyone else hear that?"

"Bird! Sounds like!"

"That was a very interesting noise."

Footsteps rang out as someone walked toward her bay. Payne took flight, panicked. "Awk!"

"There!"

"There's a bird in the studio!"

"Oh, not *again*."

"Need a broom! Chase it!"

The footsteps paused. Payne soared toward the ceiling and lighted on a rafter.

"Now everyone relax," said Grandmama's voice. "We'll leave the windows open and it'll go out again the same way it got in."

Rosa slipped out of the bay and found everyone standing in a knot, looking up at Payne.

"Crows are very intelligent birds," said Uncle Marco. He smiled at Rosa. "Some of them can even learn to talk."

Rosa froze. Had he overheard Payne talking?

"Rawk!" cried Payne. "Caw! Caw! Rawk!"

"I've got to finish this commission," said Aunt Nadia, shaking her head. "I've got no time for birds, even very elegant black ones." She hurried away.

The rest of the family began to disperse. Grandmama picked up the long pole that they used to open the high windows. "Did you clean up the drawing, Rosa?" she asked coldly.

"It's gone," said Rosa, which was the exact truth.

"Good," said Grandmama. "Now you can go get the one you drew on the back of the bathroom door. *Really*, Rosa! We just talked about this! What were you thinking?"

Rosa's mouth fell open. "I...but I *didn't!*"

Grandmama shook her head. "I don't want to talk about it. Go clean it up."

Rosa turned away to hide furious tears.

"If Rosalita says she didn't do it, I believe her," said Uncle Alfonso mildly.

Grandmama made an annoyed sound. "They didn't draw themselves!"

"Things do, sometimes," said Uncle Alfonso. "The world is a strange place."

"Don't start," said Grandmama.

When she used that tone of voice, there was no arguing. Rosa hurried from the room. That Uncle Alfonso was defending her, and she couldn't tell him the truth hurt almost as much as being blamed for drawing on the walls.

"It's such a little kid thing to do!" she said, under her breath. That was the most frustrating of all. Rosa hadn't drawn on walls since she was five, maybe less. Since before the incident with the purple-eyed cat, when she hadn't really understood about illuminations. "That was over half of my whole life ago!"

She went into the bathroom. Halfway up the door, there was another scribble. This one looked somewhat like a turtle, with a lumpy shell and crude little legs. It had far more teeth than any turtle had ever had, and huge front claws.

And if I were going to draw on walls, my drawings would be better! I could draw a much better turtle than that!

She wondered how the Scarling had managed to draw something so high up. Maybe it had stood on the edge of the sink.

Rosa didn't want to leave the drawing alone, for fear that it would vanish again, but she had to get the bucket and the sponges. *Again.* She raced to the kitchen, put the bucket under the tap, and turned it on. Then she raced back to the bathroom to check. The drawing was still there.

Back to the kitchen to check the bucket, then back to the bathroom, then back to the kitchen. It was nearly full, so she added soap and swished a sponge around. *Again.*

"Are you running laps in here?" asked Aunt Nadia, coming in for more coffee. "It sounds like a herd of horses."

"Just me," panted Rosa. She was out of breath from running. "I have to clean up the bathroom."

"Bathrooms are important," said Aunt Nadia vaguely. She seemed more interested in her coffee. "Bathrooms are the windows to the soul."

Rosa was fairly sure that bathrooms were nothing of the sort. Aunt Nadia often got a little weird when she was working on a painting, as if most of her brain was involved with art, and the bits that controlled talking were wandering around unsupervised.

"How is your painting going?" asked Rosa.

"Glorious. Terrible. I don't know. I'm a genius or an idiot. I won't be sure until it's done."

Rosa nodded. This was also perfectly normal. Aunt Nadia spent at least two-thirds of every painting convinced that she was the worst artist in the world and the other third convinced that she was best. This was slightly easier to deal with than Cousin Sergio, who believed that the painting was brilliant up until the moment it was finished, when he suddenly discovered that it was terrible and they had to stop him from setting the canvas on fire.

Rosa hauled the bucket up by the handle—*again*—and

lugged it into the bathroom. It sloshed as she walked, leaving a trail of droplets.

She reached the bathroom, turned around, closed the door, and—

The drawing was gone.

Rosa said the worst word she knew. She said it very quietly and under her breath, but she said it anyway. (She had learned the word when Cousin Sergio had tried to construct a model for a painting, using a taxidermied goat and seven silver platters, which had all fallen down on top of him at a critical moment.)

Then she kicked the toilet, hard. Her foot felt worse, but the rest of her felt slightly better.

She dumped out the water in the sink and slogged into the kitchen.

Something rattled from the top of the cupboard.

Rosa looked up.

Grandmama kept a line of painted plates in holders along the top of the cupboards. Some of them were illuminations, but most were simply things that Rosa's grandmother had acquired in her travels—plates with windmills and bridges and little shepherdesses with improbably fluffy sheep.

(Rosa rather liked them. The rest of the family claimed to hate them. "Hideous kitsch," said Aunt Nadia. "Not the good kind."

"Old-fashioned! Very!" said Cousin Sergio.

"You two will touch those plates over my dead body," said Grandmama, "and then who will do the cooking?" The plates stayed.)

One of the controversial plates rocked in its holder, and something stepped out from behind it.

It was the Scarling.

It was bigger than she'd expected. It was the size of a large rat, at least, but its limbs were dry and gray and withered looking. It looked like old tree roots or mummified skin.

The face, though...

It was a nasty, scowling face that the artist had painted, stark white with shocking red lips, like a clown. It had no eyes, but Rosa got the feeling that the Scarling could see her just fine.

Its bright red lips parted. Rosa caught a glimpse of peg-like teeth. Then it snickered.

The Scarling's voice was surprisingly deep and unsurprisingly horrible. Rosa hadn't realized that she was backing up until her shoulders hit the wall.

The empty bucket banged against her knees. If the Scarling came after her, could she hit it with the bucket?

It had something black in its right hand. Rooty fingers twined around a wavy stick half as tall as the Scarling itself.

That must be the charcoal.

The Scarling scrabbled down the side of the cupboard and landed on the counter.

Rosa's first thought was to run. She squelched that down, hard. *I have to catch it. I have to.*

...how?

It came toward her, walking on three root-like legs, holding the charcoal in the air. It giggled again, and Rosa bit her lower lip to keep from yelling or screaming or crying or all three.

It threaded its way past the narrow lip of the sink, advancing on her.

The bucket, thought Rosa. *I'll put the bucket over it and then I'll find Payne and we'll shove it back in the box.* She braced herself against the wall. *Just let it get a little closer...*

It jumped.

Rosa swung the bucket and hit the Scarling in midair.

THWOCK!

Her heart stuttered in her chest. It dropped to the floor and she tried to flip the bucket over and slam it down, but the Scarling was a hair too fast. It ran toward the stove on three shaky legs.

"No!" cried Rosa. She slapped the bucket down again, but it was too late.

She heard rattling behind the stove...and then silence.

I missed. I almost had it, but I missed.

Rosa sat down, hard. Her legs felt wobbly.

Eventually she stood up. She was reluctant to put the bucket away, but she couldn't really carry a bucket with her everywhere.

I have to tell Payne.

She closed the cupboard door and turned away, just in time to hear Aunt Nadia screaming.

FOURTEEN

Afternoon
Velvetleaf Day
Thermidor, the Month of Heat

"My painting!" shrieked Nadia. "My painting! *Rosa, what have you done?*"

Rosa dropped the bucket and ran into the main studio. "What? Aunt Nadia? What's going on?"

Aunt Nadia was standing in the doorway of her bay, with her hands over her mouth. Her face was bone white. "How *dare* you, Rosa?"

"What?" asked Rosa, bewildered. "I didn't do anything!"

Nadia pointed.

Rosa went into the bay and felt her stomach drop. It felt like it dropped clear through the floor and into the basement.

The great painting for the Merchant's Guild, the painting with eleven different angels, the painting that was supposed to help restore the Mandolini fortunes—had been defaced.

There were charcoal scribbles over the feet of the angels, and along one side. The Scarling would have had to climb up the side of the painting and lean out to draw on it, but draw it had. The face of the rightmost angel had a mustache and a beard and the eyes were blacked out and a little face, all fangs and hair, was scrawled over the angel's shoulder.

"*Rosa,*" said Grandmama behind her. "Rosa, how *could* you?"

Rosa gaped at her. "But...but I didn't! I was in the kitchen— I haven't even been here—"

The Scarling must have attacked the painting while Aunt Nadia was in the kitchen getting more coffee, Rosa realized. Then she had probably dawdled, talking to Cousin Sergio, and come back to the scene of destruction while Rosa was trying to catch the Scarling in her bucket.

It's so fast. How is it moving so fast?

She didn't have time to wonder.

"You *know* how important this is," said Grandmama. "What's gotten into you? Nadia, can you fix it?"

Aunt Nadia wouldn't even look at Rosa. "No. Maybe. I don't know."

"But I didn't *do* it!" cried Rosa. Why didn't anyone believe her?

"I don't want to hear it, Rosa. Go to your room."

Uncle Alfonso came into the bay as Rosa fled from it. She was too blinded by angry tears to avoid him, and her shoulder ran into him as she ran.

"Careful, Rosalita," he murmured.

She let out a single frustrated sob and dodged around him.

She flung herself on her bed. Payne had vanished again, and that only made her cry harder.

She wanted to tell everyone everything, right now, no matter what Payne said—but what would she say? *It wasn't me, it was a horrible little magic monster I released, but I haven't caught him, so I don't have any proof, except that the talking crow who isn't here right now says so!*

Nobody would believe her. And it *was* her fault, even if she hadn't drawn on the painting herself. She'd let the Scarling out of the box.

What hurt the worst was that she'd been so determined to help. She had been trying to improve the Mandolini fortunes, and it had all gone so very, very wrong.

"I should never have opened that stupid box," she said bitterly into the pillow. "Why did I think it would do anything good?"

"No idea," said Payne. "Humans are weird about boxes. You can put a giant sign on a box saying *Open this and the world will end and your face will be eaten by badgers* and people would line up to get a crack at the lid."

Rosa sat up, sniffling. Payne was perched on the iron frame of her bed.

"It got Aunt Nadia's painting," she said, wiping her eyes.

Payne snapped his bill, making a hollow sound. "The big one with all the angels? Ouch. It'll feed well off that one."

"You—Payne, what's on your foot?"

The crow looked guilty. "Nothing." He had one foot pulled up against his feathers, and it was wrapped in metal and glass.

"That's not nothing!"

"...something."

Rosa gave him her sternest look.

"...it was *shiny*..." muttered Payne.

It was, in fact, a tangled up mess of costume jewelry. He'd gotten his left foot completely knotted up in it. Rosa had to sit there and carefully unwrap the little links, while Payne stared at the rhinestones and made small chirps of awe.

"Look at it...look how the light catches it...like a thousand glorious diamonds..."

"It's glass," said Rosa shortly. "Cousin Sergio was using that as a model for the mermaid's treasure in his painting. And you can't keep it."

Payne looked hurt. "I'll put it with the other shiny things! To keep them safe!"

Rosa wanted to scream with frustration. "Forget the shiny things! The shiny things aren't in danger! I told you, it got Aunt Nadia's painting!"

She felt like crying again. She wasn't sure if she was furious or sad or both, and Payne was not helping.

"Sorry," mumbled the crow. He tried not to look at the jewelry. "I get distracted. It's a crow thing. Shiny goes right to my head."

"Forget shiny!" Rosa snatched the necklace away. "We have to tell my family about the Scarling! You can't let them think I drew on Nadia's painting."

"No!" said Payne. "If people find out about the Scarling, they'll want it for themselves!"

"Why would anyone want that awful little monster?" asked Rosa.

Payne snapped his beak shut and looked guilty. "It's complicated," he muttered, shifting from foot to foot.

"My *life* is getting complicated!" hissed Rosa. "That

painting was supposed to pay for—for everything! If it's ruined, we're going to be in big trouble! We have to tell them!"

"There's five of them," said Payne. "And if they each tell another person and that person tells another person, eventually the whole city will—look!"

Rosa followed the direction of his wing and gasped.

Climbing across her desk was a...*thing*.

It wasn't the Scarling. This was...well, it was...

"Is that a *drawing?*" whispered Rosa.

Payne nodded.

It was made of lines, but the lines changed as it moved, so that it resembled a dark gray dust bunny. It was flat in places, then spiky, then flat again. Looking at it made Rosa's eyes water, and yet it seemed oddly familiar.

"It's a scribbling," whispered Payne. "They can't see very well. It probably doesn't know we're here yet."

He gathered himself up.

"What do we—"

Payne pounced.

The scribbling must have realized that something was wrong. It scurried sideways. The drawn lines moved like centipede legs, incredibly fast, and it shot out from under Payne's talons and bounded up the wall.

"*Rawwk!*" Payne slapped at it with his wing and it dodged away, jumping onto one of Rosa's radish drawings. For an instant, backed against the paper, the scribbling looked like a regular drawing again, and Rosa recognized it.

It was the drawing from the hallway that had vanished.

Rosa gasped.

The scribbling missed its footing and fell off the radish drawing. Payne caught it in his beak and grabbed for it with one foot. He yanked at the lines, ripping with his claws, and it came apart into a spray of charcoal dust—and then was gone.

"There!" said Payne happily. "That'll teach it! It's hard to catch them, but they come apart pretty easily once you've gotten a grip on one." He dusted charcoal off his claws and looked pleased with himself. "Good to see that being stuck on a box for a couple centuries hasn't dulled the old beak at all."

"Rosalita?" called Uncle Alfonso. "Is the crow in there?"

Payne's look of triumph faded. "He heard me!"

"You did caw awfully loud," said Rosa. She went to the opening of the bay. "Yes, Uncle. It landed in here. It's...um...not hurting anything. I think it's hungry."

Uncle Alfonso nodded. "I shall put out some bread," he said, and vanished into the kitchen.

"But—" whispered Payne.

"Look," hissed Rosa, "everybody knows there's a crow in the studio! Just pretend to be a regular old crow and nobody will know you can talk!"

Payne fluffed up his feathers. "I suppose you're right. And bread would be good," he admitted. "I think I've earned some bread after that."

Rosa knew that Uncle Alfonso was looking for an excuse to come into her room and talk to her. He believed her, but somehow that made the fact that she couldn't tell him even worse.

"There," said Payne. "You saw that. That's what happens when the Scarling draws with the charcoal. It steals the magic from illuminations by drawing on them and then it uses that magic to make scribblings come alive. *That's* why people would want it. They could use it to make paintings that come alive themselves."

"Like you?" said Rosa.

Payne looked uncomfortable. "Probably not nearly as good," he muttered. "Tybalt was a genius. Obviously. Anyway, the charcoal is like a...a conduit, right? It takes power from one thing and moves it somewhere else. From an illumination to a scribbling."

"That's horrible," said Rosa. "Why would anyone *want* that?"

"Well..." Payne scraped his beak. "It had its uses. Look, you know how you make a sketch and then you paint over it, right?"

She nodded.

"Well, if you drew your sketch and then the Scarling traced over it with its charcoal, and then you painted on top of that, your painting would come to life when you were finished. That's why people want it. You just need the charcoal and a smidge of talent and you could make things come alive."

Rosa considered this. "You mean you could make a scribbling?"

"Much more than just a scribbling. The Scarling's not an illuminator. If you combine the talent of an illuminator with the charcoal, you get life." He snorted. "Also the Scarling just can't draw very well. It's only good at tracing."

The idea that you could make a living painting was fascinating, but also somewhat alarming. You *could* make beautiful things, like Aunt Nadia's angels, or even Uncle Marco's gorgeous beetles with their rainbow-colored shells. Beautiful things that made the world better. Then she thought of the siren painting in Cousin Sergio's bay, with her lovely scales and her long, sharp fangs. *Not nice! Eats people!*

The Mandolinis were one thing. But if just anybody could draw a painting, and have it come to life...the scribblings were bad enough. What if somebody wanted to draw really big wicked things...monsters, nightmares, devils?

The cathedral in the center of town had a gigantic painting across the ceiling. It was Art, not an illumination—illuminations weren't allowed in the cathedral, except for little ones at the doors to keep out mice—but it showed heaven and hell. The artist had clearly been very enthusiastic about painting hell. It was full of lost souls and things with extra heads and gigantic teeth *and what if somebody could make paintings like those come to life and they came walking down the street with their teeth gnashing and their claws ripping—*

Rosa began to understand why Payne didn't want to tell anybody about the Scarling.

I wouldn't ever draw anything like that. I'd draw...well, fanged radishes, probably. She stifled a sigh. She didn't know why it always came back to the radishes. She drew horses sometimes, too, but even then she usually had a fanged radish riding on its back.

If I had a charcoal like that, it wouldn't matter that I don't have my magic yet.

Way down deep, where she rarely allowed herself to think about it, was the fear that she might never get any more magic. She might never be an illuminator. But if she had the Scarling's charcoal, would that matter?

If we could make living *paintings, everybody would know that the Studio Mandolini are the greatest family of illuminators in the city. We'd never have to worry about getting enough work again. And Serena would have to take back the mean things she said.*

"If we catch the Scarling, is there a way that we can use the charcoal to make paintings without—"

Payne didn't let her finish. "There!" he squawked. "There, you see? *This* is why it's dangerous. You find out about it and you want it!"

"I was just asking!"

"Sure, that's how it starts," said Payne. "But it always goes bad. Tybalt knew it and he locked the thing away in a box and set me to guard it!"

"But—"

"People see that kind of power and they want it and they won't stop until they get it!"

"Don't yell at me!" snapped Rosa. "I didn't do anything! I just asked a question!"

"It was a stupid question!"

"You're stupid!"

"No, *you!*"

They glared at each other.

It was exactly like fighting with Serena. And like fighting with Serena, there was really only one thing to do.

Rosa stuck her tongue out and went "Nyyyyuuhhh-*uh!*"

(This had worked on Serena for years, until she had started to say, "Saints, Rosa, you're such a *child.*")

Payne fluffed up the feathers along his neck until he looked like a bottle brush and said "NYUUUHH-HUH!"

They stared at each other a moment longer, and then Rosa dissolved into giggles.

"Hmmph!" said Payne, smoothing down his feathers and looking smug.

And then everything was fine again...at least, until the next drawing showed up.

FIFTEEN

Morning
Melon Day
Thermidor, the Month of Heat

GRANDMAMA DIDN'T EVEN BOTHER to say anything this time. She simply dropped the bucket and the sponge at Rosa's feet and walked away.

Rosa stared at it. She didn't even know where the drawing was—but if she asked, there was going to be yelling. There was a hard set to Grandmama's jaw, as if she'd been pushed much too close to the edge and was going to start pushing back.

The payment from the Dynast for the great tile illumination had arrived that morning, and that should have eased Grandmama's mind a little, but it had been followed immediately by the man who sold canvas, who needed paying. Canvas was not terribly expensive, but they used a great deal of it in the studio. And then the grocer came to the door, and the woman who supplied coffee.

"They can smell money," said Grandmama, as another knock came on the door. "Jackals!

"They are mostly our friends," said Uncle Alfonso mildly. "We've known Martin for forty years."

"Do not be reasonable at me," said Grandmama. "I am not in the mood to be reasoned at. Take what's left and go pay the taxes, will you?"

"Certainly," said Alfonso. "I shall take Rosa with me."

"Rosa is grounded," said Grandmama.

"I shall not let her out of my sight," said Uncle Alfonso. "We shall have no fun whatsoever and I will not make even one joke."

Rosa hastily shoved the bucket of water back into her bay. The drawing would vanish soon anyway, like all the others, so it wasn't as if she was shirking.

He said something else to Grandmama, too quietly for Rosa to hear, and then Grandmama said, "Fine, see if you can get anything out of her, then."

"Put on your shoes, Rosalita," said Uncle Alfonso. "We have a grim duty ahead of us and I require your company."

Rosa had one sandal on when there was yet another knock on the front door.

Grandmama threw her hands in the air. "Are we to have no peace today at all? We have no more money, so they will simply have to go away!" She stalked to the front door and opened it.

They were too far away for Rosa to catch more than a few words, but her name was one of them.

"...no...Rosa...grounded...not today..."

The voice that came back was unmistakably Serena's. "Not for that. Dad sent me to borrow some pigment. He said Marco's white is the best, and he needs it for the dragon's eyes."

Rosa looked up at Uncle Alfonso in horror. She didn't want to see Serena right now. Not when she was already grounded and Serena had said such mean things to her. She had too much on her mind already and if she had to start thinking about whether or not she and Serena were still friends, she was going to collapse into a heap and wail in despair.

Uncle Alfonso patted his pockets and said, "Hmm, it seems I've forgotten my...err...lizard. I shall go look for it directly. We'll leave in just a few moments."

"Lizard?" whispered Rosa.

"Very important, lizards. One should never go out without a lizard. You never know when you'll need one." He tapped the side of his nose.

Rosa drew back into the corner of her bay and waited, listening to Uncle Marco rummage around for white paint and hand it over to Serena. "With my compliments to your father," he said.

The front door opened and closed again. After a moment or two, Uncle Alfonso returned.

"Did you find a lizard?" asked Rosa, shoving her other foot into her sandal.

"Hmm? Oh. Do you know, there does not seem to be a lizard in the place? I suppose we shall simply have to risk needing one. Now let us go."

Rosa scurried after her uncle. Grandmama watched them go with her lips pinched and an odd expression on her face.

"Now, we must be very serious," said Uncle Alfonso. "There shall be no giggling, and absolutely no joking."

He gave her an exaggeratedly somber look under his eyebrows. Rosa would have giggled under other circumstances, but she was much too worried about the Scarling.

Payne can watch things while I'm away. It will be fine. I hope.

She was torn between relief at getting away and a gnawing sense of dread that things would get even worse.

At least if I'm not home, they can't blame me for any new drawings!

They trudged along together. Rosa took two steps for every one that Uncle Alfonso took.

"Your trouble must be very serious, Rosalita," he said, when they had gone several blocks.

She grunted.

"That was an excellent grunt. You would make a very good little old man with a grunt like that."

She smiled involuntarily, and Uncle Alfonso, watching her closely, smiled too.

It was a long walk to the little office where they paid the taxes. The streets were full of people doing their shopping before the afternoon heat. Everywhere that Rosa looked, she saw people.

And under their feet and over their heads, painted on walls and ceilings and floors, on the bridles of horses and the sides of carriages, worked into lamp-posts and set into shop doors, she saw illuminations.

Some were ancient and worn away and probably hadn't worked for centuries. Some were so new that the paint shone as if it were still wet.

What would happen if the Scarling got out and began

scribbling over all those illuminations, the way it had on Nadia's?

There were illuminations on every doorway against fire and flood. Those kept the city safe. You had to have them on every building, by order of the Dynast. And there were all the other little illuminations that weren't as important, but which kept things running smoothly: the painted bridles that kept horses from slipping on the stones and hurting themselves; the shop windows etched with dancing leopards in the corners, an illumination against breakage; even the windowsills with little charms to keep pigeons from pooping on them.

Rosa tried to imagine a city without them and felt her heart sink even farther.

Maybe it won't be so bad. Payne obviously likes to yell "Doom!" It's just one nasty little vegetable, how much damage can it do? It can't draw a scowly face on every illumination in the city!

Rosa remembered the horrible painted face on the mandrake root and the way that it had advanced on her, trying to scare her. And it had been drawn immediately to the most important thing in the studio, Aunt Nadia's great angel painting.

The Scarling didn't have to draw on all the illuminations, just the important ones. The ones against fire, say. Or even the ones against pigeons.

Rosa's parents had died in a fire long ago, when she was a baby. A building behind the studio had been abandoned, and the wards against pigeons had lapsed. So the pigeons had pooped all over the building, including on the illuminations that kept away fires. It sounded funny, but the fire had raged through the building and jumped to the studio. The studio's own illuminations had burned out trying to stop the blaze.

Grandmama wouldn't talk about it. Uncle Marco had said once, very softly, that it was lucky that it had struck the studio out of all the buildings in the city. "Our illuminations kept it from spreading," he said. "Half the neighborhood might have burned down otherwise."

"Lucky for everyone but us," said Uncle Alfonso, and Rosa had slipped away so that neither of them knew she had overheard.

He had happier things than fire on his mind now. Uncle Alfonso called out to friends as they walked, waved to other illuminators, and bowed very deeply to a little old woman who waved him off with her shawl and said, "Away with you, flatterer!"

Rosa trailed along behind him. Her feet seemed to get heavier with every step.

They went into the office of the Dynast, a large, handsome building with pillars and illuminated murals that glowed with magic. None of them were from the Studio Mandolini. The magic felt silvery to Rosa, and a bit furry. Studio Lasrina, probably.

She knew that people who weren't illuminators didn't feel magic the same way, but there was so much inside the building that she didn't know how anyone *couldn't* feel it.

She hoped that feeling it meant that she was going to become an illuminator when she was older, but there were no guarantees. Grandmama wasn't an illuminator, but she had enough talent to feel a little bit of magic. She said that Studio Lasrina's paintings always made her feel vaguely as if she had dog hair on her clothes.

Rosa wandered over to a mural while Uncle Alfonso talked to the man behind the marble counter. The mural was ten feet tall and featured a parliament of owls holding scrolls and scale balances. They were very somber owls, as suited a place of government, but the branches had smiling faces hidden in them.

Uncle Alfonso finished his transaction and came back over, sighing. "Well, that's that," he said. "The money comes and the money goes. Let's go home."

A block or two from home, Uncle Alfonso paused. There was a little park, barely more than a bench and a tree, but he drew her into it. "Sit with me a moment, Rosalita. My old legs are tired."

Rosa sat beside him, staring at the cracked brickwork under her feet.

"Is there anything you need to tell me, Rosalita?"

She swallowed. She didn't dare look at him.

"Sometimes things seem very bad in our heads, but they aren't so bad when we tell other people."

She wanted to tell him so badly, but if she did, Payne would be furious. And Serena wasn't speaking to her and Aunt Nadia was so angry she couldn't even be in the same room, so Payne was the only friend she really had right now.

Even that might not have stopped her. Rosa knew that her family weren't the sort to want the Scarling's power, no matter what Payne thought. But she also knew she should have told someone right away. If she'd told her family about the Scarling when it first appeared, then they could have caught it before it ruined Nadia's painting. If an illumination held a piece of the painter's heart, then the Scarling had taken a bite out of Nadia's, and Rosa had let it happen.

If Payne and I can catch the Scarling, it'll all stop. It'll be okay again. Everything will go back to normal.

She didn't let herself think of what might happen if they didn't succeed. How much would the Scarling destroy? *And it will be my fault, because I let it out.*

Besides, the worst that happens if I don't *tell is that I feel bad. The worst that happens if I* do *is that somebody takes Payne apart to find out how he works.* You couldn't really compare the two, could you?

"All right," said Uncle Alfonso, when she had been silent for much too long. "If you think of anything...anything at all... you know I'll listen."

Rosa nodded. If he said anything else, she was going to cry.

But he didn't say anything else. Instead he stood up and they went home, past all the illuminations, which—for now— still worked.

SIXTEEN

Very Early Morning
Ryegrass Day
Thermidor, the Month of Heat

Rosa woke up in the middle of the night because there was a beak in her ear.

"Guhhnn! Whuh? Payne?"

"There!" whispered the crow, with satisfaction. "You're awake!"

"I am now," she grumbled. "You poked me in the ear!"

"Yeah, well, you sleep like a log. A *stone* log. And you snore."

"I do not!"

"You do so! Worse than Tybalt, and he sounded like a herd of elephants. Now keep your voice down and come with me!"

Rosa sat up. The studio windows were still velvety black.

"Wh...what time is it?"

"Late," said Payne. He hopped up onto her shoulder. "Midnight, at least. The Scarling's been up to mischief. Come on!"

Those words were enough to get Rosa moving. She threw her jacket on over her nightgown and padded barefoot out of the bay.

The studio was very dark. The only light on was in Cousin Sergio's bay. Sergio kept odd hours, but he was very quiet when working during the night, so as not to wake up the rest of the family.

Rosa crept up the stairs to the roof. Payne spread his wings to keep his balance as she went.

At the top, she pushed the door open a crack and slipped through.

There was no moon tonight. The lights from the city below were just enough to see by. They cast reddish shadows over the rooftop garden.

One of the potted plants had been overturned. Dirt spilled out onto the roof tiles and basil leaves were scattered in all directions. Rosa groaned. "Did the Scarling do that?"

"Probably the scribblings helped," said Payne. "If you get enough of them together, they're pretty strong. That's part of why the Scarling makes them, so they can do mischief for it."

"I don't know why it's bothering knocking over potted plants," grumbled Rosa. She scraped dirt back into the pot with the side of her hand. The sweet scent of bruised basil leaves filled the air, but Rosa couldn't really enjoy it.

Payne frowned. "That's a good question..." He hopped around the overturned pot. "Stop!"

Rosa stopped, surprised.

"There's an illumination on the bottom!" Payne sounded surprised.

"Yeah?" said Rosa. "It keeps off bugs, I think, or maybe that's the one that keeps the pots from breaking. If it's a leopard, it's for breaking, and I think the one that keeps off bugs is a burning ladder—"

"Forget the bugs!" cawed Payne. "It's been scribbled!"

Rosa groaned. She leaned over, and sure enough, Payne was right. The outlines of a burning ladder were just visible through a drawing that looked like a toad doing an interpretive dance.

"That's why they knocked it over," said Payne. "To get to the illumination."

"I'll wash it off," said Rosa glumly. "Although if we just wait, I guess it'll go away on its own."

"It'll take the illumination's power with it," said Payne. "And make a more powerful scribbling. Get rid of it now before it comes to life!"

There was a rain barrel on the roof to water the plants. Rosa couldn't find a rag, so she used the hem of her nightgown. She soaked it in the water, then scrubbed at the charcoal, smearing it.

"Why didn't the stuff on Aunt Nadia's painting go away?" she asked. "Shouldn't it have turned into a scribbling?"

Payne shook his head. "The Scarling was trying to drain it, but it was too powerful," he said. "The painting, I mean. The Scarling's still weak from all that time in the box." He saw Rosa's blank look and snapped his beak. "Let me think. Um. Straws. Do people still use straws?"

"Of course we do."

"It's been two hundred years! Maybe straws are out of fashion now!"

Rosa rolled her eyes. Payne rolled his right back at her.

"Anyway," he said, "the Scarling's charcoal is like a straw. You can suck water through a straw but you can also blow air out through it, right?"

"I guess?"

"When the Scarling drains a painting, it's drinking the magic out of it. Then when it draws the scribblings, it's blowing magic back out through the straw. That's why you couldn't just take the charcoal yourself and draw something with it. You'd have to be able to blow magic through a straw. Tybalt could do it, but nobody else could. That's why some people would do anything to get their hands on the Scarling."

Rosa was still skeptical that anyone would try that hard to get their hands on an evil carrot, but she let that go. "What does that have to do with Aunt Nadia's painting?"

"So your aunt's painting was too much to drink!" Payne waved his wings dramatically and nearly fell over backwards. "Boom! Like if you dumped a pitcher of water over your head and tried to drink it with a straw as it fell over you. The Scarling drank but instead of draining the painting completely dry, it got a little bit and made a huge mess!"

"It's a mess, all right," said Rosa grimly. "But what's it doing with the magic it *does* catch? From the little illuminations."

Payne shrugged. "Feeding on it," he said. "Blowing it back out to make scribblings to make trouble for the Mandolinis. That sort of thing. It's not complicated."

"I still don't know why it wants to make trouble for us!" Rosa dabbed angrily at the remains of the scribble. The burning ladder was still in one piece, but her nightgown was never going to be the same. "Did Tybalt make somebody really angry and they sent the Scarling after us?"

"There's another scribble over here," said Payne, pointing.

"Ugh!" Rosa righted the potted basil and went to investigate. Sure enough, there it was. The illumination that prevented the roof from leaking had sprouted teeth and three glaring eyeballs and what was either horns or tusks.

"I'm glad it takes a while for these to come to life," she said, trudging back to the rain barrel.

"Living is hard," said Payne. "Even with magic it takes a little time to sort everything out." He eyed the drawing. "Anyway, if everything the Scarling drew came to life immediately, it'd be really hard to paint over the top, so T—the person who initially made it made sure there was a delay."

"I wish they'd never made it!" said Rosa angrily. "What did the Mandolinis ever do to them?"

Payne launched himself into the air, wings beating. Rosa finished scrubbing off the second scribbling. She was getting cold and her nightgown was wet and gray from charcoal. The night air smelled vaguely of the canal, though not nearly as strongly as it had a week ago.

At least those illuminations are still working! Because I really don't want to have to go clean those off!

"Payne?" She looked around. "Where'd you go?"

The crow landed next to her. His beak was powdered with charcoal dust. "Scribbling," he said. He wiped his beak off on her nightgown, leaving long black smears. "It was going down the side of the building."

"Was it trying to get someone else's illuminations?"

"Maybe," said Payne. "But the scribblings can't get too far from the Scarling. It has to keep feeding them magic or they starve. And I don't *think* the Scarling will go far from the studio."

"Why not?" asked Rosa.

"This is where I am," said Payne simply. "And it's still mad at me."

"What did you do?" asked Rosa.

The crow gave her a look. "Helped jam it into the box," he said. "And then guarded that box for two hundred years. I suspect it's a little bitter."

"When Grandmama sees this nightgown, she's going to be more than a little bitter," said Rosa. "Can we go back in? Are there any more up here?"

Payne rolled his eyes. "Humans and their clothes. You'd be better off if you had feathers."

Rosa would have really liked to argue the point, but she had to stifle a jaw-cracking yawn, then another one.

"Go to bed," said Payne. "I can watch for scribblings."

"But what if there's more of them?"

Payne rolled his eyes. "You're as bad as Tybalt. He never wants to go to sleep when he's working eith—"

He stopped in mid-word, closing his beak with a click. After a moment he said, "Never wanted to go to sleep. When he was working. Before."

Rosa winced.

"I keep forgetting he's dead," said Payne quietly. "Like he's just gone somewhere else, where I can't talk to him."

Rosa nodded. After her parents had died, sometimes she'd forgotten that they were dead. It was like the idea was in her brain, but it hadn't gotten all the way down to her heart yet. "It's been two hundred years," she said, as gently as she could.

"For you. It was last week for me." The crow's feathers

drooped. "Whatever happened to him, I wasn't there to help him."

"I'm sorry," said Rosa, and she was. However miserable it was having her family mistrust her, it wasn't as if they'd vanished forever, without even a chance to say goodbye.

"Yeah," said Payne. "Me too." He fluffed his feathers out. "You should go to bed. I think I'll just stay up here for a while."

Rosa wished that there was something she could say to help, but she was pretty sure there wasn't. No one had ever been able to say anything to help her. She went slowly downstairs to bed, leaving Payne perched on the edge of the roof, gazing out over the city.

SEVENTEEN

Morning
Ryegrass Day
Thermidor, the Month of Heat

SHE WAS in trouble the next morning. Another scribble had appeared, on the front door this time.

"Rosa..." said her grandmother, sounding less angry than baffled, "what is the point of this? Did you get up in the night just to draw on the door?"

"*I didn't do it!*"

Grandmama rubbed her forehead. "Then why was your nightgown sopping wet and covered in charcoal?"

Rosa opened her mouth and closed it again.

"I found it in the hamper this morning," said Grandmama

wearily. "And I found the drawing when Master Roberts came over to pay for his minotaur painting."

Rosa fought back tears. "I'll clean it up," she whispered, staring at the floor.

"I already did," said her grandmother. "Now go to your room and..."

There was a knock on the front door. Grandmama sighed and went to answer it.

Rosa watched from the front of her bay as Grandmama took the minotaur money and handed most of it to the woman in the doorway, who supplied the coal to keep the stoves going. She ducked back as Grandmama turned away. She didn't feel like talking right now.

"We've got to stop this," she said to Payne, sitting on the bed with her knees pulled up to her chest. "I'm getting in so much trouble! You've got to tell them!"

"It'll stop if we catch the Scarling," said the crow.

"But we still don't know how to do that!" Rosa leaned her forehead on her knees. "How did you catch it last time?"

"...um," said Payne. He stuck his head under his wing and began preening the tiny feathers at the base.

There was another knock at the front door. Grandmama said a moderately bad word and stomped across the floor.

"Payne..." said Rosa.

"Tybalt did it," mumbled the crow into his pinfeathers. "He told the Scarling....um....something it wanted to hear. So then it came to...uh...well, it was mad, but it wanted to...err...look, it's a long story."

"I'm grounded," said Rosa. "I'm not going anywhere."

"I should check the roof..." Payne said, still not meeting her eyes.

"Payne!" Rosa glared at him. "You want me to keep a secret, but you won't tell me this?"

"Three can keep a secret if two of them are dead," said Payne. "That's a quote. Somebody famous said that. I don't remember who."

"*I'm* going to be dead if we don't stop these scribbles from showing up!"

Payne heaved a sigh. "Fine! Look, the Scarling doesn't like *me*, okay? We're both living illuminations. Except that I'm made of paint and it's not, so I'm better."

"Why is paint better?" asked Rosa.

"Than mandrake root? Have you seen a mandrake? They're icky. Whereas I am *impasto*."

Rosa knew that *impasto* was a technique where paint is applied very thickly to create raised textures. When Payne puffed up his feathers, they did look quite a lot like *impasto* painting.

"Also I can talk," added Payne, apparently as an afterthought. "Which is helpful. Anyway, it resented that. It can't talk. So I was playing dead—I am a very good actor, you know—and the Scarling went to draw a scribble on me and drain out my power, and the Scarling had its charcoal out and then WHAM!" He snapped his beak together, making a hollow clack. "Into the box!"

"But why didn't Tybalt destroy it?" asked Rosa.

"I told him to," Payne grumbled. "He never listens. Listened." He trailed off with a small chirp of distress.

SHE REACHED out and hesitantly stroked the back of Payne's neck. He sighed and leaned against her hand, like a small feathered cat.

Suddenly Uncle Marco's voice rang out through the studio, making both of them jump.

"Everyone, I think you need to come and see this. Especially you, Rosalita."

Afternoon
Ryegrass Day
Thermidor, the Month of Heat

THEY ALL CROWDED into the kitchen. Grandmama looked angry, still, and Aunt Nadia's eyes were rimmed with red, as if she had been crying.

That frightened Rosa a little, because Aunt Nadia never cried. Even when she was very angry, Nadia would only drink more coffee. Uncle Marco always said that no one could drink coffee more wrathfully than Aunt Nadia.

Rosa's stomach was tight. She looked around, but couldn't see anything was amiss. Then Uncle Marco pointed up.

On the line of plates, across the windmills and the bridges and the shepherdesses and the illuminations, were scribbled dozens of angry faces.

Rosa took a step back, half-expecting them to come to life, but they didn't move.

"Rosa—" said Grandmama, sounding even more angry than before.

It was Uncle Marco who cut her off. "Interesting," he said. "Since Rosa's been in her room all morning. And particularly interesting, because if it was Rosa, how ever did she reach them?"

Grandmama glared at him. "She must have stood on a chair."

Marco smiled. "Let's test this, shall we? Rosa, dear, get a chair and stand on it."

Rosa's face felt hot, but she fetched a chair from the table and put it against the counter. She was very aware that everyone was watching her.

She climbed up on the chair and tried to reach the plates.

Uncle Marco laughed, but not at her, because Rosa was at least two feet too short, even with the chair. Her fingertips didn't come anywhere near the top of the cupboards.

"She couldn't have done it," said Uncle Marco. "It would have been very unlike her anyway, but she couldn't have drawn them."

"I don't think she could have drawn the other ones either," said Uncle Alfonso. "Rosalita's an artist, and no artist worth the name would have done that to Nadia's painting."

Rosa had to blot her eyes again after that. She climbed down carefully. She didn't look at Grandmama, because she wasn't sure what she'd see.

In the end, she didn't have to.

Grandmama reached down and hugged her tightly. "Oh, Rosa..." she said, and her voice cracked a little. "But your nightdress—"

"I was trying to clean one up," said Rosa. "Before you saw it."

"Oh, my dear, I should never have doubted you. I was wrong, and I apologize."

Aunt Nadia reached out and squeezed Rosa's shoulder. From Nadia, that was as good as a hug.

"I'm sorry," she said. "I was so upset—but of course you wouldn't. Even when you were very small, you never *ruined* things like that. You were always trying to help."

Rosa started to cry again, out of sheer relief. Having her family mad at her had been terrible.

And then somebody asked the question that she was dreading.

"But if Rosa didn't do it, who did?"

EIGHTEEN

ROSA GULPED and wiped her eyes. When she had calmed down a little, she found that everyone was looking at each other, and no one was looking at her.

They don't expect me to know. Nobody is waiting for me to answer.

"Now that's an interesting question..." said Uncle Marco.

"A vandal?" asked Aunt Nadia doubtfully.

"Art critics!" cried Cousin Sergio. "Nasty!"

Uncle Alfonso shook his head. "I'm not sure we're dealing with a human here," he said. "This seems more like unkind magic."

"That," said Uncle Marco, "is an even *more* interesting thought."

Cousin Sergio climbed up on the chair and took down one of the plates. He put his thumb on it and frowned, then went to the sink and washed it. Then he frowned again.

"Feel!" he said, shoving it at Aunt Nadia. "Feel it!"

Nadia took it and her face, too, twisted up in a frown. She silently passed the plate over to Grandmama.

When it had gone through every hand, it came at last to Rosa.

It was a plate.

Only a plate.

It took a moment for that to sink in, and then she gasped.

Painted across the ceramic was a bright golden fish wearing a crown. It was meant to keep flies away. Even as old as the plate was, it should have had the faint, misty feeling of an illumination.

But it was only a plate.

"The illumination's gone," she said.

"Drained!" said Cousin Sergio.

"Like it wore out," said Uncle Marco. "Now that *is* interesting...and a bit frightening."

"Alfonso? You're the only one who's dealt with wicked magic before," said Grandmama.

Rosa's ears pricked up.

"Dear me," said her uncle. "That was so long ago...and I was young and foolish..."

He glanced around the kitchen, but apparently found no escape. "Perhaps you could put on some coffee, Aunt?"

"I shall," said Grandmama, "but don't stall. You can talk while it brews."

Uncle Alfonso sighed. "There's so little to tell," he said. "I was sent off to study with one of the masters. Donato, it was. This was in the fifteenth year of the new calendar, you understand, and he was still grumbling about it. *'Thursday!'* he used to shout. *'It's Thursday! Don't give me this nonsense about Bryony Day!'* A long time ago now, and the Mandolini fortunes were also not...ah...doing so well. Most of the promising young men had gone off to war and my cousins had gone to be nurses and not everyone came back."

"I came back as soon as I could," muttered Uncle Marco.

"Of course you did. It wasn't your fault. Well. My mother and my aunt were holding the place together as best they could, but they had no time to teach me. I was too young to fight, so I had to go apprentice to a master."

He sat down in a chair, while everyone else crowded around.

"Donato was a fierce old fellow, and he had two apprentices. Myself, and a young man named Francis. I am afraid...well."

He looked down at the table. Grandmama poked him in the shoulder. "You're doing no good by being modest, Alfonso. I remember him."

"Francis had a good eye," said Alfonso. "But he was impatient with himself. That's one of the hardest parts of being an artist, you know—learning to be patient with yourself when you're not as good as you want to be. You have to say, 'I may not be very good today, but I'll be better tomorrow, and in a year, I'll be amazing!' But Francis couldn't do that. He just saw how good our master was—"

"And you," said Grandmama.

"And me," said Alfonso, and sighed. "I was a quick learner, that was all. He would have caught up. But he was impatient, and he started experimenting with illuminations to make himself better."

"But what's so bad about that?" asked Rosa.

Uncle Alfonso smiled ruefully at her. "It's an important question. You can't really use magic to make yourself better at magic. It's your own gift that fuels the paintings, and so you could only make yourself as good as you are already. It'd be like trying to stand on your own shoulders. But once you start changing yourself, you open the door to all kinds of other changes. Francis..."

He sighed again. Grandmama slid the coffee in front of him and gave him a stern look. "Fewer sighs, Alfonso! The past is past. We need facts now, not regrets."

"Very well," said Alfonso. He took a sip of coffee. "Francis painted illuminations to change himself, but he didn't always paint them quite right. He painted an illumination to make himself remember lessons better, but instead he remembered *everything*. He couldn't forgive anyone for even the least of slights after that, because every time they talked, he'd remember everything they'd ever said all over again. He couldn't sleep because of the memories. And then he'd paint an illumination to sleep better, but that one changed his dreams instead, and he'd paint another one to rid him of nightmares, and then he wouldn't dream at all. If we don't dream for too long, we get angry and confused. And eventually he fixated on the person he thought was his chief rival—"

"Was it you?" burst out Rosa. "It *was* you, Uncle, wasn't it?"

"Yes, Rosalita, it was. And he got a book from somewhere, of forbidden illuminations—paintings that hurt and harm and unmake, instead of paintings that help people. He began painting illuminations to sabotage mine. It was...well, it was really quite ingenious. He painted these terrible forbidden illuminations and he tattooed them on the backs of rats and he would let the rats go in my studio. We had both graduated by this point, so I had a studio of my own, but all these little plagues and misfortunes were being dragged all over it and I had no idea what was happening."

"What happened?" asked Aunt Nadia. "How did you find out?"

Uncle Alfonso shrugged. "One day I left some cheese out, and actually saw one of the rats. You notice a shaved rat with a painting on its back, believe me! So we set out traps and caught them, and then it was easy to tell that it was Francis' work. So Donato and I went to confront him."

"Did he fight you?" asked Rosa. She pictured a grand enchanter's battle, brushes flying over canvases, illuminations being flung at one another—

"No," said Uncle Alfonso. "He was very scared and sad and he hadn't slept in days. I think he was a bit glad to get caught. He was wearing a coat covered in the paintings that kept changing him all the time. When we took it off him, he collapsed. We burned all the wicked illuminations and Donato disposed of the forbidden book. An order of nuns took Francis in and cared for him, but he never held a paintbrush again. Though I always felt very badly for the rats. They hadn't asked to be used like that."

Uncle Alfonso sat back in his chair and finished his coffee. He gestured to the line of plates, covered in their nasty scribbled faces. "Anyway," he said. "That's what these remind me of. The rats getting everywhere with their wicked illuminations. Except that rats couldn't draw, so I'm not sure if this is really all that much like it after all."

THE MANDOLINIS DISPERSED, still talking. Grandmama took down the remaining plates to wash them herself. Rosa wondered if any of them were going to come alive—no, surely soap and water would take care of that. They seemed to vanish quickly enough when the sponge passed over them. She went back to her bay, thinking of rats and paintings.

She wanted to tell her family all about the Scarling. She almost had. But now that they weren't blaming her for the drawings, surely it would be easier? She just had to catch the Scarling, that was all.

Payne crawled, grumbling, out from under the bed. "You're back, then."

"Why were you under the bed?"

"I was...um...doing something...."

"Did the *something* involve shiny things?"

"That is completely irrelevant," said Payne. He scowled as well as one could with a beak instead of lips. "It is possible that shininess was involved, but I don't see how it matters."

"Never mind that," said Rosa. She hurriedly explained the Scarling's attack on the plates. "It drained them all! And how did it get there so fast?"

"It's in the walls, I think," said Payne. "Like one of those rats your uncle was talking about."

Rosa frowned. "How did you know that?"

"I may have been eavesdropping," Payne admitted. "Your Aunt Nadia had a spoon that looked like the moon cast in silver plate, like a mirror of heaven, like—"

Rosa folded her arms.

"*Anyway,*" said Payne hurriedly, "the Scarling has to come out to feed on the illuminations. We'll just have to keep an eye out for where it's likely to be."

This proved easier said than done.

NINETEEN

Ram Day to Safflower Day
Thermidor, the Month of Heat

FOR THE NEXT THREE DAYS, Payne and Rosa watched for the Scarling and things went steadily, desperately wrong.

It did not tackle any of the big paintings again. Perhaps it had over-exerted itself. But all the little household illuminations, one by one, began to vanish under the onslaught of charcoal. There were so very many illuminations in the house, and once the Scarling had drawn on something small, the magic was gone. The illumination failed at once, even if Rosa got to it before it became a scribbling.

"It's feeding on the magic," Payne said. "The only reason that big one of your aunt's is still working is because it was too powerful. The Scarling's eyes were bigger than its stomach."

The kitchen was the hardest hit. The little green sun that helped the bread to rise went first, and then the one that kept the milk from spoiling and the one that kept the garbage from stinking. The blue-eyed cat painting in the pantry sprouted horns and fangs and scrawled wings and mice came in and rioted over the cheese.

"I don't know what this is," cried Grandmama, dragging the garbage away, "but it has got to stop!"

Rosa nodded glumly. In high summer, the garbage smelled horrible. She hadn't realized how much those little illuminations mattered.

Everyone in the studio reacted to the crisis in their own particular ways.

Aunt Nadia drank coffee until she slept only in five-minute intervals, and she refused to leave her painting for even a second. Uncle Marco had to come in and watch the painting while she used the bathroom. She was carefully lifting out each charcoal mark with a palette knife and repainting the angels underneath, even while her hands shook from too much coffee.

Cousin Sergio stood on his head until he passed out, trying to get enough blood flow to make his brain work properly. Grandmama forbid any more headstands, so he took to roaming the studio armed with a walrus tusk that he had found in the basement, randomly striking at shadows in case of art critics.

Uncle Marco took down reference books, laid them open, and zoomed around the bay on his stool, from book to book, looking for clues about what was going on. He had seven books open at various points along the beetle painting, and Walter had to dodge flying bookmarks.

Grandmama cooked when she was upset. As the illuminations failed—and as Sergio and his walrus tusk racked up an

increasingly large pile of broken crockery—she cooked more
and more.

Baking was her chosen refuge. Several of the failed illuminations affected the way that dough rose and kept pies from
burning. This made Grandmama more upset, which made her
bake even more. By the end of the third day, every flat surface
in the kitchen was covered in pies and Rosa had been sent out
to the neighbors with a delivery of baked goods.

"Ah," said the elderly man who did laundry for most of the
families along the street. His house was spotlessly clean and
smelled of soap. "Trouble at home, I see."

"How did you know?" asked Rosa.

"Mincemeat pie in midsummer? Your Grandmama only
cooks like that when she's upset."

"I've got three of them," said Rosa wearily. There was an
illumination painted on the threshold. All the dust fell off her
shoes when she stepped through the door.

She was relieved that the laundry illuminations were still
working correctly. It was bad enough that the Scarling was
wreaking havoc in the studio. If it got out and started bothering
strangers...

Rosa thought she'd die of shame. And worse, the
Mandolinis had painted most of them, so if people thought the
illuminations had failed, they'd go somewhere else for replace-
ments—Studio Magnifico or Studio Lasrina. The Mandolinis
couldn't afford to lose any work. And what if the Scarling took
out the illuminations to protect against fire, and someone got
hurt?

"Oh, marvelous," said the laundry man, snapping her out of
her reverie. "I'll take them. I hope your Grandmama feels

better, of course, but if some lemon tarts get made before then, I'll be happy to take them off your hands."

Rosa delivered six more pies and a plate of pastries. Every illumination she saw seemed to be working, except for one. That one was supposed to ward off spiders, but it was older than Rosa and the owner was notoriously cheap, so it had probably just worn out. She ducked under the cobweb draped over it and headed home.

More baking had taken place in her absence. It was swelteringly hot in the studio with the oven going, and they had to open all the windows. (Payne went in and out several times. He said that the city had grown enormously in two hundred years and it was all very unsettling.)

"I think I saw a rat," said Uncle Marco, picking his way between pies. "I tried to hit it with my cane, but it was too fast. Did whatever-it-is get the ward against rats?"

"No, I think that one's still good," said Grandmama. She leaned against the counter with a cookbook. "Lingonberry. Have I done anything yet with lingonberry?"

"I'm quite certain I saw something rat-like," said Uncle Marco.

The illumination that warded off rats was a painting of a flaming wheel with a snake in the middle. It was painted on a big tile inset in the middle of the floor, and when people walked over it, it was supposed to "turn the wheel" in a magical sense, and make it even more powerful, like a waterwheel turning a millstone. Illuminations based on wheels were usually put on the floor for just that reason, although the one to ward off rats was the most common. If you painted a roasted chicken instead of a snake in the middle, it would ward off peacocks, but very few people were ever overrun with peacocks, so it didn't come up much.

Rosa suspected that the reason the Scarling hadn't gone for the rat illumination was because it was right out in the open and people would have seen it. On the other hand, that meant that Uncle Marco probably *hadn't* seen a rat, but the Scarling itself, or one of the awful living scribbles.

She found an excuse to prowl around Uncle Marco's bay, but didn't find either. Walter the beetle waved his antennae at her as she went by.

When she emerged from the bay, she was promptly handed a set of berry tarts. "Take these next door."

"But I already took him mincemeat."

"Lingonberry will go well with mincemeat. Now go!"

Rosa bowed to the inevitable and took the tarts next door.

"Back so soon?" said the laundry man, accepting the tarts. He smiled. "Well, that's good. One of my illuminations in the back seems to have failed, and I was going to come and tell you about it anyway."

Rosa's heart sank. "Show me," she said. "I'll...err...tell my grandmother..."

"So odd," he said, leading the way into the back of the laundry. A big copper boiler stood there, where he heated the water. Underneath was a metal box where he built the fire, and it was inscribed with illuminations of winged snakes all around it to prevent the fire from throwing sparks.

At least, it was supposed to be illuminated that way.

The charcoal drawings were badly smudged. It looked like the laundry man had tried to clean them off. Enough remained that Rosa could see that the Scarling—or at least one of the scribblings—had been here.

She knelt down and touched the painted snake. One of Uncle Marco's, she thought absently. Had a scribbling come out of it?

"There was some sort of stain on them," said the laundry man, peering at her near-sightedly. "I must have dropped dye on it. I tried to wipe it off, but it doesn't seem to be working now. Sparks everywhere! My own fault, though. If you could ask someone to come and touch it up, I'd be very grateful."

Rosa stood up. "Let me see if I can get the rest of the dye off." She was amazed how calm her voice sounded, when her insides felt squeezed with dread. She wanted to scream.

It was happening. Just as she'd feared. The Scarling had gotten out of the studio and was unmaking the illuminations.

TWENTY

Afternoon
Safflower Day
Thermidor, the Month of Heat

"Now, we don't know that the Scarling is going out that far," said Payne later, while Rosa drank hot chocolate in her bay and tried not to cry. "It was probably a scribbling. I think the Scarling'll stay close to the studio."

"But how do we know that?" demanded Rosa.

"The Scarling hates Mandolinis," said Payne, waving his feathers negligently. "I hoped maybe I could lead it away, but I'm pretty sure it won't leave until it's driven the studio into the ground."

"Payne—" Rosa gulped. "What if it tries to burn the studio

down?" It was the thing she feared most. Her parents had died in a fire. If the Scarling took all the wards against flame down...

"It won't," said Payne. "It's made of wood and paint. It's afraid of fire, too."

"But one of its legs is charcoal!"

"Yes, and if your leg got burned off, you'd be pretty wary of fire after that, wouldn't you?"

Rosa exhaled. Payne was right. "The scribblings are drawing on everything, though."

"The scribblings just like ruining things. The illuminations mostly still work if you can clean them off."

"Yes..." admitted Rosa. She'd salvaged the laundryman's illumination in the end. "But only because it was painted on metal and I could get the drawing off." It had taken her nearly twenty minutes to clean it off with a dry paintbrush. The charcoal had gotten into the grooves in the metal and she had to be very careful not to take the paint up by scrubbing too hard. "What if one draws on something that I can't clean?"

Rosa knew, as all artists must, that what you draw *on* can be as important as what you draw *with*. Metal and ceramic were one thing. If the scribblings had drawn over an illumination on paper, she would be left trying to erase the drawing. It would probably tear and there would certainly be big black smudges where everything had been ground into the paper. And if the charcoal was on paint on a canvas, it might depend on the kind of paint and the canvas would certainly be gray and dingy and scruffy looking, assuming she could get the drawings to come off at all.

"This could be bad, Payne."

"Yes, but at least it's just scribblings. They're single-minded little monsters. The Scarling wants to eat the magic. It's more discriminating." He shook his head. "It might go into some of the buildings around the studio, but it won't actually leave. Not until the Mandolinis are...uh...well."

"Ruined," said Rosa morosely.

"That, yes."

"If we told my family, we could have everyone watching for it."

Payne snapped his beak. "Tybalt told somebody, and one of them must have told somebody else and apparently they wrote a book about it and I will bet you a fresh tube of lapis blue paint that it was the very same book that Francis person found and made so much mischief with. And you want to tell *five*? No, no, and no!"

"You still haven't told me *why* whoever made it hated the Mandolinis so much!"

Payne sighed. "Tybalt made some bad decisions," he admitted grudgingly. "He was very smart and he knew it and he tended to think that made him right. Occasionally he made an enemy."

"Did he murder somebody?"

Horror crossed the crow's face. *"No!* Of course not! Tybalt was *good!"*

"It's just that it's stayed mad for two hundred years—"

"Yes, and it's probably forgotten why it was mad. Now it's just furious because it was locked in a box for two hundred years by the Mandolinis."

This was a fair point. And it didn't really matter why it was mad, since Rosa wasn't going to just give it the studio, even if it had a really good reason. "Fine," she muttered. "But give me back my spoon!"

Payne, who had been trying to make off with the spoon

from Rosa's hot chocolate, made a sad sound. "But it wants to be with the other shiny things!"

"No, it doesn't," said Rosa. "Spoons don't *want* things. And you're just lucky that Grandmama thinks the vanishing spoons have something to do with what's going on, and doesn't suspect you."

She stomped back to the kitchen to deliver the liberated spoon. Unfortunately the silverware drawer was blocked by a stack of muffins, so she had to put it in the sink instead. She snagged a muffin on the way out, though. It tasted of blueberry and anxiety.

It was a shame that the Scarling wasn't shiny, she thought grimly. Otherwise Payne would have snapped it up within ten minutes. Instead the wicked mandrake root was still causing havoc *and* Cousin Sergio had been complaining about how someone kept moving the jewelry he was trying to paint.

I just wanted to improve the family fortunes! she thought. *And now things were much worse than before and the studio stank and the one person who was supposed to be helping kept getting distracted by costume jewelry and spoons!*

It was the worst week she could remember having for a very, very long time.

"I AM OUT OF LAPIS BLUE," said Uncle Marco. "I need it to finish off the last of the beetle shells."

Grandmama sighed. "We don't have any?" she asked. The illuminations that kept the roof from leaking had fallen prey to scribbling the night before, and she was grimly putting out buckets while Cousin Sergio tried to paint a new one.

"Not a drop," said Uncle Marco. "Not a dollop. I have checked with everyone."

"Did you check Sergio's bay yourself instead of just asking him? You know how absentminded he is."

"He is completely devoid of lapis paint," said Uncle Marco. "His last three skies have been painted grey because of it. I had thought it was an artistic exploration of the nature of clouds, but actually he's out of blue paint."

"We can't afford more," said Grandmama. Lapis blue was terribly expensive and had to be made by powdering gemstones.

"Then the commission will go unfinished," said Uncle Marco, folding his arms. "Walter will have modeled in vain."

Grandmama rubbed her forehead wearily. "Rosa, run down to the Studio Magnifico and ask if they can spare a smidgeon of lapis blue. We loaned them a great deal of red ochre when they were doing that dragon for the chapel wall, and that white paint just the other day."

"Going!" said Rosa happily. She was excited to get out of the studio without an armload of pies. Payne was moping around in the rafters, supposedly looking for the Scarling but probably just trying to find shiny things to swipe for his collection. He was not very good company at the moment, and sooner or later they were going to run out of spoons entirely.

She was halfway down the street before she remembered that she and Serena still weren't on speaking terms. Her footsteps slowed.

Still, Serena had come to her studio to get paint. It wasn't charity, it was just what studios did for each other. She would be very polite and very mature and perhaps if she was very lucky, Serena's brother would answer the door instead.

When she knocked on the door of the Studio Magnifico, however, Serena opened it.

Rosa opened her mouth to say, very maturely, that her Uncle Marco had requested to borrow some paint, but Serena was faster.

"Oh, thank goodness!" she said, and grabbed Rosa's wrist. "You're here! Maybe you can tell me how to stop it!"

TWENTY-ONE

"...HUH?" said Rosa, but Serena was already dragging her into the bedroom.

Serena's bedroom was in shambles. It was never terribly neat, even at the best of times, but it looked as if someone had torn it apart. The sheets were piled in the middle of the bed, the drawers were hanging open and everything on top of the dressers had been swept onto the floor.

"Whoa," said Rosa, standing in the middle of the wreckage. "What *happened?*"

"What?" Serena looked at her, then around the room. "Oh! That. I did that. I was trying to find it!"

"Find what?" asked Rosa, who was starting to get a sinking feeling in her stomach.

"Whatever's drawing all over my stuff!" said Serena, and shoved a jar into Rosa's hands. "Look! It's like the thing that happened at your house!"

Rosa looked down at the jar. It had a gryphon painted carefully on the lid. She recognized the gryphon immediately—it was the sort that Serena usually drew, the way that Rosa drew radishes—but she had to admit that Serena had done a very good job on it. It was clearly an illumination, though it wasn't very powerful. Rosa could feel the magic against her fingers. Serena's magic felt like faint, fuzzy velvet. When her friend grew into her power, Rosa thought, her magic would feel like thick, soft fur.

Unfortunately the gryphon now had a mustache and glasses drawn on it and there was a long flappy tongue sticking out of its beak.

"Someone did this at your studio too, right?" said Serena. "I saw the drawing on the door when I came for white paint!"

Rosa shook her head slowly, not because Serena was wrong but because she didn't know what to say. This was worrying. More than that, it was *weird*.

The Scarling was still at the Studio Mandolini, or at least close by it. It was still leaving drawings everywhere. Surely it couldn't have come all the way here? How long did it take a mandrake root to walk anywhere, anyway?

"When did this start?" asked Rosa.

"Night before last," said Serena. "I didn't know what to think. But whoever it is only got two of them, but then last night they came and drew on some of the others! I had the jars that weren't ruined hidden and they didn't move them but they drew all over them! And I was asleep in here the whole time!"

It has to be a scribbling. It must have gotten here somehow. Maybe it rode over when Serena picked up the paint. This was a much better thought than that the scribblings were traveling multiple blocks on their own. "There's...um...something going on at the studio, yeah. Drawings on stuff." She ran her finger around the edge of the jar. "The illumination still works," she said with relief. "It's still magic." If it had been the Scarling, the gryphon wouldn't have been anything but a painting. Probably. Unless Serena had started cleaning it before the drawing had a chance to work.

"Well, *yeah,*" said Serena. "I painted it! And a bunch more like it. This thing's drawn on four of them, though. It's pretty awful. I worked really hard on those!"

Rosa squirmed inside with guilt. Serena wasn't always a great friend, but she was Rosa's friend, and this had been her very first commission. Commissions were important. They were more important than some stupid thing Serena had said a week ago. And Rosa was the one who had opened the box, and that made what the Scarling did her fault, so it was almost like Rosa had ruined the drawings.

A few days ago, she'd been horribly jealous of Serena's commission, and somehow that made the guilt even worse.

"What's doing it?" asked Serena. "Do you know?"

Rosa stared down at the gryphon.

Payne had told her not to tell anyone. But Payne was back at the Studio Mandolini and Serena was right there, looking at her.

She stared at the gryphon for so long that Serena said "Rosa...?"

"Crayon," said Rosa abruptly.

"Crayon?" said Serena. "What do you mean, crayon?"

"It's in crayon!" said Rosa, laughing with sudden relief. "The scribble! It's in crayon!"

"Well, yeah," said Serena. "The blue-violet one. Why?"

"It's not charcoal!" If it wasn't in charcoal, it *definitely* wasn't the Scarling's work. The scribblings might have gotten out, but they couldn't drain an illumination, just mess it up so that it needed to be cleaned.

Serena's eyebrows drew together. "Why would it be in charcoal?"

Rosa bit her tongue.

"Rosa, what do you know about this?"

"I...well..."

Serena's voice acquired the sharp, grown-up edge she got sometimes, the one that Rosa didn't like. "Rosa, if you know, you have to tell me!"

"I can't," said Rosa. "I can't. I'm really sorry. I can't."

"But—but—"

And then, to her horror, Serena dissolved into tears.

"It was my first commission!" she sobbed. "And I have to redo them and I'll be late and I'll have failed on my very first try and no one will ever hire me again. They'll know that I couldn't even illuminate jar lids! And I worked so hard on them and I *know* they're just little jars but it was a real grown-up commission!"

"Serena—Serena it'll be okay—" Rosa put her arms around her friend, horrified.

"But what if it keeps happening?"

Rosa gulped. Not telling Uncle Alfonso had been bad enough, but he hadn't cried.

"How do I keep them safe? Rosa, what do I *do?*"

"I...well..."

Payne made me promise not to tell my family, but he didn't say anything about Serena, so I wouldn't really be breaking my promise, just bending it a little.

She had a strong feeling that Payne wouldn't see it that way. But Payne wanted people not to use the Scarling's charcoal.

Serena wouldn't create monsters even if she knew how. Serena can't even think of wicked monsters, she only draws pretty things like gryphons. And I have to tell her something.

Rosa swallowed. "If I tell you, you have to promise not to tell anybody."

"I won't," said Serena, sniffling. "You know I won't. Swear on the Blessed Virgin, I won't."

Rosa nodded. Serena could be annoying and she could be bossy and she could even be mean, but she never spilled secrets. If you made her promise not to tell something, wild horses couldn't drag it out of her.

Rosa took a deep breath and then said "It's a monster. And it's my fault."

Saying the words aloud was nearly impossible at first, but as she told her friend about the box and the crow, they came out easier and easier, until she was blurting out the last words in a rush. "And a scribbling must be drawing on yours but it can't be the Scarling because it's in crayon, not charcoal!"

There. There. I told someone.

She felt as if a weight had fallen off her chest, as if she'd let out a breath that she hadn't known that she was holding.

"Well, it's awful," said Serena. Her voice was still thick and gluey, but she had stopped crying. She scrubbed tears off her cheeks with her hand. "I've had to scrape purple crayon off three of the lids. I couldn't save the fourth."

Rosa stifled a sigh. It seemed like, having finally admitted the awful truth about the Scarling, Serena should have been more impressed. Instead she was still talking about her commission.

"And the drawings didn't eventually vanish?" Rosa asked.

Serena looked at her as if she'd gone mad. "Vanish? Crayon

doesn't vanish. I had to use a palette knife and scrape the wax off."

The drawing is in crayon, and it didn't go turn into a scribbling creature, and it's still an illumination, even if it's ruined. Definitely just a scribbling.

"Anyway," said Serena, "it's in my room somewhere. I'm nearly sure of it. I saw something moving, but it was too fast. You have to help me catch it before it gets into the rest of the studio!"

"I'll help. You can't tell anyone, though," said Rosa. "It's important that nobody knows, or they'll try to keep the Scarling."

"I don't know why anyone would want to keep it!" said Serena. "It seems awful!"

Rosa nodded. Payne would have to forgive her. She couldn't very well have helped Serena without telling her at least a little about what was going on.

"All right," she said. She was surprised by how grown-up her voice sounded. "All right. I've got an idea."

TWENTY-TWO

It took them nearly an hour to set a trap for the crayon-wielding monster. It would have taken a lot less time, but Serena had locked up all the jar lids with the gryphons on them and had lost the key when she tore her room apart. So most of the hour was spent straightening Serena's room up until they could find the key.

"This is as bad as Sergio's study," said Rosa.

"When I am a Great Beauty," said Serena, sounding like her old self again, "I shall have maids and servants to clean my room. I shall live in a vast house with twenty-seven closets and I will never hang clothes up myself again."

"You'll have to marry someone very rich," said Rosa, halfway under the bed, "if you're going to have a servant for every closet."

"Naturally," said Serena.

"What if you fall in love with someone poor but handsome?" asked Rosa.

Serena paused, her arms full of papers. "My family shall forbid us to wed," she said. "I shall die tragically of a broken heart. And I still won't have to hang up clothes."

"Your family wouldn't forbid you," said Rosa. "Not because of money, anyway. They aren't like that."

"Well, they'd forbid us for some reason. Maybe he'll have a dark past." Serena, once she was determined upon a course of tragic death, was unwilling to turn aside.

"Oh! You could fall in love with a poor but handsome art critic!" said Rosa, and then had to duck as Serena threw a pillow at her.

Once they found the key at last—it had fallen into the clothes hamper—Serena unlocked the chest at the foot of her bed and took out one of the gryphon jars.

"Are we sure we have to use one of mine? It's so hard getting the crayon off."

"If it drew on four of them, it must like them," said Rosa. She tried not to feel jealous. The Scarling hadn't even touched her radishes. *Which is stupid because I don't want it to draw on my radishes! I just...wish they were good enough for it to want to...*

They set the lid down on the floor, with the gryphon facing up. Serena emptied out an even bigger jar, which was full of interesting rocks. Rosa picked one up and turned it so that the light caught the veins of quartz.

"Now what?" whispered Serena.

Rosa took a deep breath. She'd only seen a picture of a trap like this before. She turned the jar upside down and leaned it against the dresser so that it was propped over the gryphon lid.

"Do we have any string?"

"I've got ribbon," said Serena. "That's like string."

It was bright pink ribbon. Rosa felt on some level that if you were going to trap a monster, you shouldn't use bright pink. Still, sometimes an artist had to work with the materials that they had available.

She tied the ribbon around the rock—a stick would have been better, but Serena didn't collect sticks—and propped the jar up over the gryphon lid, on top of the rock.

"Now what?" asked Serena.

"Now we hide," said Rosa. She climbed onto the bed and pulled the blanket up over her head. Serena wiggled under it beside her.

From under the edge of the blanket, they watched the jar.

And watched. And watched.

"How long do we wait?" whispered Serena.

"I don't know!" Rosa whispered back. "I've never done this before!"

They kept watching.

"We could pretend we're in a jungle, setting a trap for a monster," said Rosa.

"We're in my *bedroom* setting a trap for a monster," said Serena.

Rosa heaved a sigh. This was undoubtedly true.

"Besides, you always bang around stabbing the monster with a sword when we pretend," said Serena. "And it's loud."

Rosa sniffed. "There's no point killing a monster if it doesn't know it's been killed," she said, but Serena was probably right. They needed stealth.

They watched some more.

"So my brother said you were down in the sewers for the installation," Serena said after a while.

Rosa wasn't sure if talking so much, even in whispers, was a good idea. Still, it was really boring waiting for something to happen.

She remembered how excited she'd been to be able to tell Serena about the installation. It seemed like it had been years ago now. She'd wanted to rub in the fact that she'd been there. But now she and Serena were actually talking again, and she didn't want to ruin it. Payne was already going to be furious with her, so who knew if there would be anyone but Serena to talk to?

"Yeah," she said, as quietly as she could. "It was pretty neat. The illumination started glowing when they put it all together. I've never seen one glow like that before."

"They glow when they're really powerful," said Serena loftily.

"Yeah, but have you ever seen it?"

"Well...no. But everybody knows that."

Rosa doubted that *everybody* knew this, but Serena couldn't see her rolling her eyes from under the blanket. "Whatever. Anyway, it was interesting. You should have come."

"I heard it smelled really bad."

"They gave us little masks. And then it worked and the smell went away." She remembered the filth in the water, how it had looked for an instant like a giant serpent, and how the golden light of the illumination had banished it. "It was—"

"Shh! Look!"

Rosa froze.

Across the floor, crawling like an injured centipede, was a scribbling.

It was a little bigger than Rosa's hand. It looked terrible. It was faded and washed out. The one that Payne had pounced on had been crisp, sharply drawn, and angry. This one was blurry, smudged, and seemed to have difficulty walking.

It was dragging a purple crayon.

"It's going for my gryphon!" hissed Serena.

Rosa elbowed her. "Quiet!" she whispered.

The scribbling paused. It didn't have eyes, exactly, but Rosa still got the impression that it was looking around blearily, then it focused on the gryphon again.

She didn't breathe at all as the scribbling approached the jar.

Come on...come on...just a little farther...

At the opening to the jar, it paused. Rosa bit her lower lip. It reached out a wavy black line and touched the ribbon-wrapped rock, as if puzzled.

Then it gave a wavering shrug and slipped under the jar, onto the lid, pulling its crayon behind it.

Rosa yanked the ribbon.

The rock popped out from under the jar. The jar fell down. The scribbling was trapped inside.

She pounced on it in a move that would have done Payne proud, pinning the lid shut. The scribbling inside slapped at the glass with the crayon, leaving smudges of wax, but nothing more.

"Is it a bug?" said Serena. "What *is* that thing? It's got— legs? Something?"

"Scribbling," said Rosa. "One of the things the Scarling makes. I *told* you."

"The Scarling? The thing you said was in the studio? Really?"

"Yes!" said Rosa, frustrated. "Weren't you listening?"

It is extremely aggravating to spill a secret to someone who then turns around and says, "What?" Rosa had not realized just *how* aggravating.

"Yeah, but I thought you were just telling stories."

"Serena," said Rosa severely, "this is important! These things are loose in the Studio Mandolini and you can't tell anybody, but we have to stop them! They'll draw in crayon on every illumination in the city!"

Serena might be an occasionally frustrating friend, but she was an artist and the daughter of artists. She blanched at the thought. "What?! No!"

"Right," said Rosa. She shoved the jar into her bag. "I have to take this back to Payne so he can kill it."

Serena stood up. "I'm coming with you."

Rosa blinked at her.

"Look," said Serena, "you're my friend, okay? Even if you're weird sometimes. And you've got monsters in your house! And apparently they could get all over everything, so we have to stop them. I'm going to help."

"Oh..." said Rosa faintly. She had been doing this alone, with Payne—who didn't really count—for days. Having another kid along who might understand would be...well, it would be a lot easier. She felt a little bit as if she might cry. "Oh."

"Besides," said Serena practically, "that stupid thing drew all over my gryphons!"

She paused and took a deep breath, staring at the floor. "And look, I want to say I'm sorry. I was awful to you the other day, and I didn't mean it."

"Oh," said Rosa. "Oh, right. Okay." Truth was, in her panic over the Scarling and Payne, she'd almost forgotten about it.

"The Mandolinis aren't crazy," said Serena. "I mean, not

any more than all artists are. And I shouldn't have said it." She scuffed her foot on the floor.

"Why did you?" asked Rosa, interested.

"I don't know!" Serena scowled. "Well...I do know. Your aunt got the commission for the Merchant's Guild painting. And my father thought he was going to get it. And I guess I was mad for him."

Rosa frowned. "Your family gets commissions we don't, though."

"I know that," said Serena, sounding a bit annoyed. "But I said something to my dad, and he said—look, we're going to be taking commissions forever, right? And sometimes you'll get one and I won't, and I'll get one and you won't. Dad said I had to learn to deal with it and that's just how it is sometimes. You can't get mad at the other artists." She scuffed her foot. "And I know he's right. But sometimes I just say things when I'm mad and it's mean and I know it's mean and I don't *want* to say them but I also sort of *do,* and I know it's wrong and I'm sorry. I keep trying not to. I don't want to be that sort of person. I don't *want* people to have to keep forgiving me." She squared her shoulders and looked Rosa in the eye. "But I was mean. Will you forgive me?"

This seemed very complicated. Rosa wasn't entirely certain how to feel about Serena wanting to say mean things. On the other hand, Serena didn't admit to being wrong very often. "I forgive you," Rosa said, and carefully did not say that she had been very jealous of Serena's commission to paint gryphons.

They shook hands on it, like grown-ups.

"Right," said Rosa. "Let's get to work. And I need some lapis blue before we go."

TWENTY-THREE

PAYNE WAS PERCHED in her studio, looking innocent, which undoubtedly meant that he had made off with another spoon. Rosa stomped into her bay with Serena behind her.

"Payne," she said, "this is Serena."

"Caw?" said Payne.

"Don't play dumb. I told her about you."

"Caw!" He looked furious. All his feathers stood up and he snapped his beak. "CAW!"

"I had to." She reached into her bag and pulled out the jar. "Look what was in her studio!"

The crow wavered for a moment, eyeing Serena, then folded his wings and hopped down onto the desk. "Caw," he muttered sulkily.

Rosa set the jar carefully on the desk. She could tell that Serena was staring at her, even without looking, and her cheeks felt hot. What if Payne refused to talk?

The scribbling looked even worse than before. It lifted the

crayon weakly, tapping it against the glass. Rosa almost felt sorry for it, but then she thought of it drawing furiously over Serena's gryphons—her friend's first real commission *ever*—and the surge of pity died.

"It drew on her illuminations," said Rosa. "But they didn't stop working."

"Now that's interesting," said Payne.

"You can *talk!*" squeaked Serena.

"Yes, well." Payne looked embarrassed. "Nobody's going to believe two kids. They'll think you're playing make-believe. So I suppose it's safe enough to talk to you."

Rosa glared at him. The fact that he was right did not change the fact that it wasn't fair.

Serena turned to Rosa. "Everything you said was true, then?"

Rosa threw her hands in the air. "How many times do we have to do this? Why doesn't anyone ever *believe* me?"

Payne ignored her, peering at the scribbling in the jar. "It's got a crayon," it said thoughtfully. "And you said it was trying to draw. Huh."

"It scribbled all over my gryphons!" said Serena indignantly.

"The Scarling draws on illuminations to drain them," said Payne. "Like Rosa's aunt's painting. It's trying to feed on the power of the illumination, and its charcoal lets it tap into that. Once it's got the power, it can sort of push it out to its scribblings. But a scribbling can't do it by itself, and they certainly can't do it with a crayon."

He tapped the glass with his beak. The scribbling waved its crayon in weary threat.

"Does *it* know that?" asked Rosa.

Payne paused with his beak half open. "You know, that's a good question. They aren't smart. I mean, they're mostly driven by instinct. More like cockroaches than crows."

"Maybe all it knows is that you draw on things to eat them," said Rosa. "So it tried doing that. It wasn't smart enough to know you need magic charcoal."

Serena looked from her friend to the crow and back again. "So it was trying to eat my illuminations?"

"Maybe," said Payne. "The scribbling must have climbed into your bag or latched onto your shirt or something, then hitched a ride to your studio." He frowned as well as he could with a beak. "Which is worrisome, but one scribbling by itself is mostly just a nuisance. It's when they get into groups that they start to get dangerous."

"I thought you said they'd stay close to the Scarling!" said Rosa. "They could be all over the city!"

Payne shrugged. "I suppose they could be. But the Scarling's the only one who can drain a painting to feed them, so they'll starve like this one if we can just get rid of their creator."

"But they'll keep drawing on people's illuminations!"

"Sure, but that doesn't really *do* anything, does it? They can't use the power themselves. And they'll only live a few days without the Scarling feeding them power." Payne glanced at the one in the jar again. "Of course, this one's back here now, so if it can get back to its master, it'll perk right up."

"It doesn't matter if they only live a few days!" yelled Serena, waving her hands. "Do you know how much damage they can do? That thing ruined half my jar lids! I'll have to paint a bunch more gryphons now, and I am so *sick* of painting gryphons!"

Payne gaped at her.

"I thought you liked painting gryphons," said Rosa. "You always draw them."

Serena collapsed on the bed with a groan. "It's different when you *have* to do it. It stopped being fun after about the third one. Now it's like homework. And now I'll have to draw more because the stupid scribble-thing ruined them."

Rosa picked up the jar to see if the gryphon lid on this one was ruined. It looked mostly intact, except for a few purple lines.

"The illumination still works," she offered.

"I can't give a client a lid covered in crayon marks, even if it still works," said Serena. "It wouldn't be professional. You'll understand when you're older."

"I understand *now*!" snapped Rosa. "I grew up in a studio the same as you!"

"Settle your feathers, both of you," said Payne.

Serena pursed her lips, then sighed. "Sorry," she mumbled again. "You're right."

Admitting she's wrong twice in one day? Rosa wished she had time to enjoy it. She pushed the jar to the back of the desk, up against the wall. "If we can catch the Scarling, at least it won't happen again."

"What if it's happening to other painters, though?" asked Serena. "What if one gets into my brother's paintings?"

Rosa flinched. She remembered how she'd felt about the Scarling drawing on Aunt Nadia's painting.

"We just have to catch the Scarling," she said. "We have to."

"I'm impressed you caught the scribbling," admitted Payne. "How'd you do it?"

Rosa explained the trap with the jar and the rock. "Could we do something like that for the Scarling?"

Payne frowned. "I don't know. Maybe, but it'll have to be better bait. This scribbling really liked the gryphons, apparently, but I don't know if the Scarling likes any illumination more than the rest. Maybe your aunt's angels..."

Rosa tried to imagine a jar big enough to fit over Aunt Nadia's giant painting and snorted. "We'd need a *house*."

"Could we use that thing as bait?" asked Serena, pointing to the scribbling in the jar.

Payne and Rosa both looked at her, surprised.

"Y-e-e-es...." said Payne slowly. "You know, that might actually work...these things are its troops, and it takes energy to create them. It's possible that it might try to get this one back..."

Rosa glanced over at the scribbling and frowned.

It was doing something very odd. It had wedged itself up against the side of the jar, away from the wall, and had propped the crayon up like a barricade. The faded lines rippled in agitation.

"It's doing something weird," she said.

She picked up the jar and the scribbling immediately relaxed and dropped to the bottom of the jar again.

"Put it back where it was," ordered Payne.

Puzzled, Rosa pushed the jar to the back of her desk again.

The scribbling immediately flattened itself back against the side of the jar.

"It looks like it's trying to get away from something," said Serena.

All three of them looked at the wall behind Rosa's desk, with its collection of pinned drawings, scraps of paper, and interesting feathers.

"Is there something behind the wall?" asked Rosa doubtfully.

Payne hopped over to the jar and began pushing it along with his beak.

Tap—tap—tap—

The scribbling relaxed again.

The crow hopped around the other direction and began pushing. *Tap—tap—*

The scribbling shoved the crayon against the far side of the jar, as if holding a spear against an enemy.

"It happens when it gets in front of that drawing," said Serena.

"Huh?" Rosa looked more closely at the wall. "But that's nothing. It's just one of my radishes."

"She's right," said Payne. "It really doesn't like that radish. And you know, now that I think of it, when I caught that other one, it was because it had jumped on a radish drawing and fell off."

Rosa sighed. She knew that Payne and Serena were wrong. There had to be something in the desk, or behind the wall. "Those drawings don't *do* anything! They're not even real illuminations!"

"Mm," said Payne. "Let us conduct an experiment, shall we?"

Rosa drew a fresh fanged radish, while Payne and Serena watched. She realized that Serena had been right—when you had to draw it, it felt more like homework than fun.

Still, once she got the outline, it got easier. She was on familiar ground. She drew long leaves and gave it a particularly fierce fanged scowl. It looked almost as ferocious as the scribblings themselves.

She set the drawing down on the floor, in front of the jar. Payne crouched on the edge of the table, ready to pounce.

There was some disagreement about who would open the jar, but Serena said it was *her* gryphon lid, so she got to do it, and Rosa had to reluctantly yield the honor.

Serena reached down and yanked the lid off.

The scribbling crept to the edge of the jar and slowly, slowly extended a single smudged line, like a finger, out of the opening.

Two girls and one crow held their breath.

The line touched the drawing of the fanged radish.

The scribbling recoiled as if it had been burned. It huddled in the back of the jar, waving the crayon threateningly. And no amount of coaxing, not even a very good drawing of a gryphon, would get it to come back out.

"Well," said Payne, looking over at Rosa. "Now we know what an illumination of a fanged radish does, after all."

TWENTY-FOUR

Night
Safflower Day
Thermidor, the Month of Heat

THEY DECIDED that it would be best to catch the Scarling at night. During the day it would be too easy for an adult to walk by, see two girls and a crow hunched over a jar, and start to ask questions.

Grandmama didn't particularly want Serena to stay over—not with all the chaos going on—but she also still felt guilty about accusing Rosa of lying, so when Rosa said, "Oh please, *please*, Grandmama?" and made her best pleading expression, she sighed.

"Fine. But after dinner, mind. I can barely cook in this mess and I won't serve someone a meal with mouse droppings in it!"

"Certainly not," muttered Aunt Nadia, from her bay. "Mouse droppings are for family only."

"Thank you!" said Rosa and flung her arms around her grandmother's shoulders.

"Hmmph," muttered Grandmama. "And you're to go to bed at a reasonable time, you understand? No staying up until dawn giggling."

"Yes, Grandmama," said Rosa dutifully.

Grandmama rolled her eyes. "I know what's going to happen," she said under her breath. "Now take the trash out. The charm's failed *again*."

It was a breathless afternoon. They ran out of lapis paint again. Uncle Marco's chair broke a wheel and nearly spilled him over, and while they were fixing the chair, another drawing appeared, this time on a cabinet. It didn't hurt anything where it was, but the sight made Grandmama extremely cross.

The man who delivered milk came to the door and asked very politely to be paid for the week.

"Half a moment," said Grandmama politely, closed the door, and turned around. "Marco! Alfonso! Nadia! Does anyone have any money? Rosa, go check Sergio's coat pockets."

"I have nothing!" shouted Nadia. "I have not even bought a cappuccino in weeks!"

There was some loose change in Sergio's coat and a crumpled-up bill. Sergio waved vaguely at her as she took them.

Between this and Uncle Alfonso, they put together enough to pay the milkman.

"If the man selling eggs comes, we are not home," said Grandmama. "We have moved to the country and then died."

Aunt Nadia emerged from her bay for five minutes, carrying a stack of paintings on coasters.

"There!" she said, slamming them down on the table. "Eleven paintings of white cats with blue eyes! We will put them in the pantry and when these *things* draw on one, we'll pull it off the top of the stack and use the next one." She scowled fiercely. "And when they have ruined all eleven paintings, I do not care if the mice hold the annual Harvest Dance on the cheeses! I will not paint another cat!"

She stomped back to her canvas.

In the silence that followed, Rosa heard Uncle Marco call, plaintively, "Has anyone seen Walter?"

"Saw a thing!" shouted Cousin Sergio. "All wiggly! Like a spider! Ran into mousehole!"

Must be a scribbling, thought Rosa. She wondered how many there were now. She scrubbed at the drawing on the cabinet, but she wondered how many she was missing. Sometimes they were too far up on the walls for her to get.

Grandmama leaned against the counter and put her apron over her face.

"We can't go on like this," she said simply. "Nothing is getting done. If someone is trying to drive the Studio Mandolini out of business, they're doing a fine job."

Rosa's heart sank as she slipped away, back to her bay. It was the very thing she'd feared and she'd helped bring it about. She had preparations to make.

If we can catch the Scarling again, everything will go back to normal. It has to! She fought down the sense of panic. There wasn't time. She had preparations to make.

When Serena came over after dinner, the chaos had been briefly contained. Rosa made hot chocolate for both of them and brought the mugs back to her bay.

"Payne!" she hissed. "We're completely out of spoons! I had to stir with a fork!"

Payne wouldn't meet her eyes. "I don't know what you're talking about."

"Give me back the spoons!"

"But I *need* them! They're so shiny!"

Rosa folded her arms and tapped her foot, the way Grandmama did when she was angry. "Payne..."

She was delighted to see that it worked. The crow mumbled something but went under the bed and emerged, dusty, with two spoons.

"I need the rest," she said.

"There aren't any more. Um. I put the others somewhere safe. You know. In case someone tried to take them."

Serena looked from Rosa to Payne. Her eyebrows were halfway to her hair.

"He has a problem with shiny things," said Rosa. She took the spoons back to the kitchen. When she returned, the fork in the hot chocolate was missing. "Oh, for crying out loud..." One of these days Grandmama was going to clean under her bed and find an entire silverware drawer. Rosa had no idea how she was going to explain that.

"*Anyway,*" said Payne, attempting to look dignified, "we have a plan. We shall use the scribbling as bait, under this box. Then when the Scarling tries to get into the box, we will slam the lid, with the painted radish, on top of it. Are we clear?"

Serena and Rosa both nodded.

"Where's the lid?"

Rosa brought it out hesitantly, hoping that someone would appreciate it.

She had spent the rest of that hectic afternoon painting the radish on the lid of a hatbox. She had to borrow paint from Uncle Alfonso, but when she told him what it was for, he had given her his very best carmine red and a smidge of titanium white.

"A great artist must have great materials," he said, when she goggled at the paint.

"But I'm not a great artist, Uncle."

He smiled. "Well, great materials can't hurt. If you give a beginner cheap paint that runs or discolors or breaks into gritty pieces, they will learn that paint is hard to use, and that is entirely the wrong lesson."

She carried the paints back to her bay, feeling honored and a little intimidated.

The important thing, she knew, was to use very little paint at first. You could always add more, but it was very hard to take it away again. "Like salt!" Cousin Sergio was fond of saying. "Only a little! More if needed!"

So she dipped the very tip of her brush in the gorgeous red paint and slowly filled in the shape of the radish. The white was next, and it stood out magnificently against the brown cardboard hat box.

It was the best thing she had ever painted. She almost forgot why she was painting. Seeing the radish come to life, with the bright white highlight to make it look like it was really three-dimensional and not flat—Rosa took a deep breath and sat back.

"I did that," she said aloud. "This is mine." She added the tiny fangs, and then mixed a little bit of Payne's gray—she was amused by that coincidence—with the red and painted shadows along the bottom and around the fangs.

She was afraid the entire time that she was going to mess

up, but she didn't. It was done and it was gorgeous and she wanted to hang it on her wall, but she couldn't.

Maybe afterwards. After we've caught the Scarling.

Now she held the lid with both hands and waited.

"Oh, well done," said Payne. He paused. "Almost an illumination, too. Can you feel it?"

"I can," said Serena. "That's not bad at all, Rosa. But the leaves are a little blobby."

Rosa gazed down at the radish. "Radish leaves are sort of blobby anyway." Thinking, *Please don't let the Scarling ruin it. I want to keep this one.*

One side of the box was open. The scribbling moved wearily in its jar.

Rosa and Serena pulled the blankets over themselves and settled down to wait. Payne lurked in the rafters, as motionless as a stuffed crow.

The lights in the studio went out, one by one, as the adults went to sleep. Grandmama walked by and glanced in, saw blanket covered shapes, and kept going. If she noticed the box on the floor, she thought nothing of it.

Blue moonlight streamed in through the high windows. Rosa's hands were sweating. She had to set the box lid down and wipe her palms on the blankets.

They waited.

Long minutes passed. The moonlight crawled slowly across the floor.

Something rustled in the shadows under her desk, and Rosa was suddenly very glad that she wasn't waiting alone.

One spindly leg at a time, like a fat-bodied spider, the Scarling inched out into the pool of moonlight.

Serena's hand closed over Rosa's wrist and gave a panicky

squeeze. Rosa wished that she could squeeze back, but she didn't dare let go of the lid now. They might not get another chance.

The Scarling looked around suspiciously. Its painted face was stark white against the dark wood of its body.

Serena made a tiny noise of disgust and the Scarling froze.

Don't move! thought Rosa, silently willing her friend not to move, not to breathe, not to make a sound.

She didn't. After a long moment, the Scarling seemed to relax. It picked its way across the floor toward the scribbling in the jar. It held its stick of black charcoal over its head like a battle flag.

The Scarling reached the edge of the box and looked in.

Come on...come on...just go inside and I'll slap this lid on you...

It stood outside the box for a long time, and Rosa began to worry. Was it too obviously a trap? A box with a jar in it? How could it be anything but a trap?

Is the Scarling smart enough to figure this out? The scribblings didn't...

It took a step inside. She saw its white face vanish into the shadow of the box.

"Now!" cawed Payne, but Rosa was already moving. She threw herself off the bed and slammed the lid sideways onto the box.

In her panic, she used too much force. The box skidded away from her, lid jammed halfway down. The glass jar clinked as it hit the leg of her bed.

The Scarling slammed against the lid, knocking it partway off—and ran into the painted radish.

A smell like burnt toast filled the bay. The Scarling

shrieked, a thin, metallic sound that went right through the middle of Rosa's head. She slapped her hands over her ears. On the bed, Serena yelled, whether from pain or to try and drown out the awful noise, Rosa wasn't sure.

The Scarling staggered and fell down. It began trying to crawl away. In the dim light, Rosa thought that she saw smoke curling from its root-like flesh.

Payne, apparently unaffected by the scream, dropped from the rafters with his talons outstretched.

Rosa heard running feet. Lights came on all over the studio.

"What was that?!"

"Murder! Fire! Thieves! Save Rosa!"

Grandmama's voice roared, *"What is going on?"*

TWENTY-FIVE

THE SUDDEN LIGHT dazzled Rosa's eyes. She couldn't see what was going on. She heard Payne cursing and the Scarling shrieked again, and then a thump and a rattle.

"Payne!" she cried. "Payne, what's happening? Did you get it?"

"Who's in pain?" shouted Uncle Marco. Rosa could hear his cane thumping against the floor as he hurried toward the bay. She knew that had to be hurting him and she wanted to tell him not to run, but there was too much going on and she didn't know what to do first.

She grabbed for the jar, with bright spots still swimming before her eyes. Her fingers closed over something hard —the lid?

And then it moved in her hand. Root limbs clawed at her fingers.

She was holding the Scarling.

Rosa let out a full-throated scream. Her first instinct was to throw the monster as hard as she could, to get the awful thing *away*.

Her second instinct was to grab even tighter so that it didn't escape.

Her fingers loosened for a critical moment. The Scarling wiggled free.

Rosa slapped her other hand over it and felt something snap.

Pain blossomed in her hand, like a dozen needles jamming into her flesh. Rosa screamed again and reflex took over. She heard a thud as it hit the wall.

Then scrabbling.

Then silence.

Gasping for breath, she looked up. The bright spot over her vision was fading.

Her family filled the doorway. Serena was crouched on the floor next to her.

"Rosa?" said Grandmama. "Are you hurt?"

"What was that thing?" asked Uncle Marco, leaning heavily against the wall.

Uncle Alfonso's eyes did not leave Payne. "Rosa," he said slowly, "do you know what's going on?"

Rosa knew that she had to say something, but she couldn't think of anything at all. What could she say? Everyone had seen the Scarling, hadn't they?

Payne saved the day.

"Caw!"

He took off into the air, circling the bay. "Caw, caw, caw!" He dive-bombed Sergio, who yelped and covered his head.

"Bird!"

"Caw!"

"It's the crow!"

"Get a net!"

"Everyone calm down!" shouted Uncle Marco, in a voice that had cut through battlefields in his youth.

Payne settled on a rafter, cawing grumpily to himself.

"Now," said Uncle Alfonso, "what is going on?"

Those few seconds were all Rosa needed. She'd tell the truth, just not quite all of it. "We set a trap," she said. "For the—the monster that's been drawing on things." She pointed to the jar and the box.

"One came to my house!" said Serena indignantly. "And Rosa helped me catch it, so then we thought we'd do it here, too."

"There's a big one," said Rosa. She didn't want to say *Scarling,* because it would be hard to explain where she got that name. "And little ones. Um, I think." (She added the *I think* so no one would ask how she knew.) "And we caught a little one, so then we tried to catch the big one with it."

"And we did!" said Serena. "Rosa grabbed it!" Her nose wrinkled. "It was gross-looking, too. Like a big hairless rat crossed with a carrot."

Uncle Marco's eyebrows drew together and he looked at Uncle Alfonso. Alfonso spread his hands helplessly. "I only saw a bit of movement," he said. "I'd have thought it was a rat. I couldn't tell you what it was. And that description doesn't help me much."

"I didn't see it very well," said Rosa hurriedly. "I mean, it was mostly dark and I grabbed it, but I thought I was grabbing the jar. It felt all...um...scabby."

"Caw," Payne grumbled.

"Right," said Rosa. "And then the crow showed up. I think

it, um, doesn't like the drawing thing? It tried to attack it. But I was still holding it. And then we all fell over each other and yelled and I dropped it."

She held her breath. Was that enough? Would they believe her? Would she get in trouble?

"That was very brave," said Uncle Marco finally.

"And foolish!" said Grandmama. "It could have hurt you!"

"It bit me," said Rosa, holding out her hand. The little wooden peg-teeth had left a semi-circle of red dents. Pinpricks of blood bloomed in the bottom.

"Tsk!" said Grandmama. "You see? Come with me, young lady, we'll clean that right up."

"But why didn't you tell us, Rosa darling?" asked Aunt Nadia, as Grandmama led her to the kitchen. "That was a good plan to trap it. We might have helped."

Rosa opened her mouth and closed it again. "Uh..."

Uncle Marco laughed. "A small group of soldiers can succeed where an army might fail, Nadia. Can't you just see us all lurking around a box with a string?"

Aunt Nadia smirked into her coffee cup. "You make a valid point, I admit. Too many painters spoils an illumination."

Serena looked puzzled. "Don't you Mandolinis ever collaborate on a painting? We do it all the time at home."

"I don't work well in groups," said Aunt Nadia. She slid down in her chair a bit. "Mine is a solitary genius."

"Yours is a genius that won't let anybody else touch their work!" said Uncle Alfonso.

"That, too."

Grandmama sat Rosa down at the table and went to work on her bitten hand. Rosa kept her other hand in her lap, in a tight fist. She could still remember the way the Scarling had wiggled in her grasp.

"Truly, we're not a collaborative lot," said Uncle Marco to Serena. "Sergio really is a genius, but it's not something he can explain to other people, and Nadia has her own way of doing things. Alfonso and I will help each other fill in large bits, but he loves great vast landscapes and I love painting little creatures, like Walter."

"My parents work on each other's paintings a lot," said Serena. "And my brother and my six cousins all work together, too."

"Nothing wrong with that," said Uncle Alfonso firmly. "You can do great things together. Look at the illuminations on the canal! But it requires a different sort of thinking." He smiled ruefully. "And I'm afraid there are fewer Mandolinis than Magnificos, too."

"There," said Grandmama, interrupting. She had sponged Rosa's hand down with stinging antiseptic, and then with a soothing cream. "And of course we're out of illuminated bandages."

"We've got some at home," volunteered Serena.

"It's two in the morning," said Grandmama. "I'm not waking your mother up for a couple of pinpricks." She glared down at Rosa. "But you tell me at once if it starts to hurt or throb or swell up, young lady!"

"It hurt when you put the stuff on it," muttered Rosa.

"That's different. Now have some cocoa and go to bed. That's enough excitement for one night."

"Yes, Grandmama..."

Serena and Rosa trudged back to her room. Rosa looked up

and saw Payne still on the rafters. He glanced down at her and sidled along the beam, waiting.

It felt like hours before the grown-ups stopped moving around. But the lights went off, one by one, and then finally Payne dropped down into the bay.

"Well," he whispered. "That was a mess. We were so close, too!"

"What do we do now?" whispered Serena.

Payne shook his head again. "I don't have any ideas," he admitted. "The Scarling won't fall for that trick twice."

Rosa slowly unfolded her fingers. She had kept her left hand clenched the entire time, afraid that someone would notice, but no one had.

There was a black smear on her fingers, and in the palm of her hand was a long, crooked piece of charcoal, and a tiny bit of root still curled around the end. The snap she'd felt had been one of the Scarling's brittle legs breaking like a twig as it tried to keep hold of its charcoal.

"We have this."

"WHAT?" said Payne. "Rosa, is that—is that the Scarling's charcoal?"

Rosa carefully took the napkin she'd held the hot cocoa with and drew a line with the thin black stick. She had to angle it into the moonlight to see what she was doing.

It looked like charcoal. It smudged like charcoal. It left little black smears on her fingertips like charcoal.

"I think so," she said. "I mean, it's charcoal, and the Scarling dropped it when I grabbed it..."

Payne began to laugh. He leapt into the air and flapped his

wings delightedly. "Rosa, I will give you all the shiny things I own! You did it! That's the most important thing! Without that, the Scarling will starve!"

"Hush!" whispered Rosa, waving him down. "You'll wake everybody up! Again!"

"Right, right." He landed on her shoulder and preened her hair.

"I don't understand any of this," whispered Serena. "What is that thing?"

"Charcoal," said Payne. "Magic charcoal. The Scarling uses it to take magic from one thing and put it somewhere else. That's...uh...how it's draining all those illumination...things...."

He seemed distracted. Rosa followed his gaze and saw that Serena had taken a barrette out of her hair and left it on the table. The moonlight was hitting it and making the paste jewels sparkle.

She put her hand over her eyes. She'd grabbed a monster, yanked its weapon away from it, possibly saved the day, gotten *bit*—and Payne was fixated on another shiny object.

"So can we use the charcoal to stop it ourselves?" said Serena. "Maybe drain its drawings first?"

"Nah," said Payne, hopping closer to the barrette. "It's a really rare...uh...skill..."

"So why are you so worried about people finding out about it?" asked Serena practically. "If nobody can use it?"

This was an excellent question. Rosa was torn between being proud of her friend and a bit chagrined that she hadn't thought to ask first.

"They might want to use the Scarling," said Payne. He tapped his beak against the barrette. "Look how it sparkles!"

"Payne! Pay attention!"

"Sorry...yeah...uh..." The crow looked away hurriedly. "I mean...what were we talking about?"

"Whether we can use the charcoal to stop it," said Rosa.

"Oh...no..." His eyes began to drift back to the barrette.

Serena snatched the barrette up and shoved it into her pocket. Payne blinked at her and scuffed his foot on the table. "You didn't have to hide it," he mumbled.

"Yes, I did! Now pay attention!"

"Ugh." Payne rolled his eyes. "Without the charcoal, the Scarling can't drain energy from the illuminations. The scribblings will starve. It can't make new ones. It'll just be an evil carrot running around. We can use your radishes to catch it and put it in the box."

"But—"

"Go to sleep in there!" shouted Grandmama. "Or I'll make Serena walk back home, see if I don't!"

"She wouldn't really," whispered Rosa. "Or she'd send Sergio with you, anyway."

"I know," whispered Serena. "But I *am* tired." She stifled a jaw-cracking yawn.

Rosa wanted to ask how she could possibly be tired, but then yawned herself. Suddenly it was as if all the excitement had worn off and she was exhausted.

They climbed into bed, and the last thing Rosa saw was Payne standing on the box in the moonlight, muttering to himself about spoons.

TWENTY-SIX

Morning
Blackberry Day
Thermidor, the Month of Heat

THE NEXT DAY brought a string of people—and trouble—to the Studio Mandolini's door.

"It's happened again," said the laundryman, wringing a towel apologetically in his hands. "All this dirt on the doorstep. I hate to ask, but you did such a good job last time..."

"Of course," said Rosa. She hurried after him, Serena hot on her heels.

The scribbling had gone to work on the illumination over the door. The painted bricks showed a smiling goat with its tail on fire, but now it had a mustache and a hat and fangs. There was a scrawled bunch of lines, as if the scribbling had tried to write a rude word but didn't know how to write.

"It's like what happened to my gryphons!" hissed Serena.

The laundryman frowned, looking from one girl to the other. "Is there something wrong?"

"No," said Rosa, grabbing Serena. "We'll clean it up in just a minute. I just need...um...supplies." She dragged the other girl out the door, leaving the baffled laundryman looking after them.

"Serena, you have to be quiet!" hissed Rosa, once they were standing out on the street. "If people find out I let this thing loose, they'll blame the Mandolinis! We'll be ruined!"

A man walked by with his dog on a leash and looked over at them, hearing Rosa's agitated tone. "No fighting now, girls," he called, in the jovial tone that grown-ups use when they think they're smarter than children.

"We aaaarrrren't," called Rosa back, in the saccharine tone that children use when they know they're smarter than the grown-up in question. She and Serena rolled their eyes at each other.

Even so, for a moment, she expected Serena to say something awful, like "Well, it *is* your fault you let the thing loose." But she didn't. She just nodded once, determinedly. "Sorry. I forgot. I won't forget again. What do we do?"

Rosa's mind was racing. "We have to go around to all the buildings around the studio. All our neighbors. And clean off the illuminations. And then..." She gulped. "We have to draw fanged radishes. Something to keep the scribblings out."

"That might be a lot of radishes," said Serena.

Rosa heaved a sigh. "Yeah. I know."

It was Serena's idea for Rosa to draw them all on little

sheets of paper so that they could simply drop off the radishes next to the existing illuminations. "They don't try to ruin the radishes," she pointed out. "They just try to get away. This is like...oh, like burning a candle to keep the mosquitoes away. The mosquitoes don't attack the candle, they just fly away. We're putting out candles."

"I wish I knew why they hated my radishes," muttered Rosa. Although after drawing about fifty of them, she was starting to get rather tired of radishes herself.

It was Rosa's idea to go around to all the houses saying that she'd made a new illumination and she wanted to test it, and would it be okay if she put one in the house? "They don't do anything bad," she assured the little old lady across the street. "And it's free. I just want to see if they work."

"Of course," said the little old lady. Her apartment was full of lace doilies and smelled like old hard candy. Rosa found the illuminations against fire on one of the rafters and placed the fanged radish drawing so that it could stand guard over them.

"You want to put an illumination here?" said the laundryman. "All right." That was the most difficult, because Rosa couldn't just draw a radish on paper and stuff it under the boiler without starting the sort of fire she was trying to prevent. They ended up putting the drawing in one of the gryphon jars and sliding it under the boiler, next to the original illumination.

Payne took radish drawings up in his beak and flew to rooftops, sliding them into cracks and crevices near the illuminations they were trying to protect. Rosa and Serena flopped down on the front step of the Studio Mandolini and looked up, watching his dark form silhouetted against the bright white clouds. Occasionally he would soar out of sight and then come down, pull another radish drawing off the stack, and fly away again.

Serena stayed over again that night. They were both exhausted from going around to all the houses and asking if they could put in a free illumination.

"What does it *do?*" asked Miss Lupe, who had three small yappy dogs and a very large, very warlike tomcat. "This illumination?"

"It should keep the other ones from getting dirt on them," said Rosa, which was more or less true, if you approached the truth sideways and squinted a bit. "So they last longer."

"Oh! How useful!"

The tomcat eyed her lazily as she placed the illuminations. There was an odd smudge of soot on his white nose...or was it charcoal?

"Did you catch a scribbling?" asked Rosa softly. "Did you think it was a mouse?"

The tomcat blinked his golden eyes at her and looked smug.

To reach the neighbors behind the studio, they had to go around the block. "Look!" said Serena. "Or...well, I guess *smell!*"

Rosa sniffed. A street vendor was selling something that smelled delicious. A man walked by wearing so much cologne that it made her nose wrinkle. "What am I smelling?"

"You're *not* smelling the canal!"

"Ohhh..." Despite everything, Rosa lifted her chin proudly. She was part of the Studio Mandolini and they had helped to fix the canal. Beside her, Serena looked just as proud.

A moment later, she saw Payne overhead, surrounded by a crowd of frantic pigeons, and reality came crashing back down. "We've still got to stop the Scarling," she said. "Or else eventually it'll eat those illuminations, too." She thought of the great lashing snake in the dark. If the Scarling ruined the illuminations that cleaned the water, people might drink it before they realized what was wrong, and they could get terribly sick or even die.

And it would all be Rosa's fault.

Night
Blackberry Day
Thermidor, the Month of Heat

ALL THREE OF them collapsed in Rosa's bay that night. "No giggling all night," said Grandmama wearily. Rosa thought that she might not have let Serena stay over at all, except that she needed someone else to eat all the baked goods. They took a plate of lemon tarts and retreated from the kitchen.

"So we've maybe protected the illuminations," said Rosa, eating a tart. "That's important." She felt very responsible, having tried to protect all the people who depended on the Mandolinis for their illuminations. "But it still doesn't stop the Scarling."

"Uh-huh," said Payne. He was staring at a barrette in Serena's hair. There was a sparkly pink glass flower on it.

"We've got to find a way," said Serena. "Do you still have the charcoal?"

Rosa nodded. She'd kept it in her pocket the entire time they'd been wandering around. It seemed like the best way to keep it safe, since the Scarling was staying close to the studio.

"You're sure it's going to stay in the studio, Payne?"

"Studio," he said agreeably, not taking his eyes off the glass flower.

"If I give you the barrette, will you concentrate?"

"Yes," said Payne. "Absolutely. Of course." He watched as Serena unsnapped the barrette, fascinated. "Oooh...so shiny...."

She set it down in front of the crow. He bounced up and down on his clawed feet, admiring it. "Caw!"

"Now, Payne. The Scarling," said Rosa.

"Scarling," he said, nodding, not looking anywhere near her.

"Payne." Rosa snapped her fingers.

"Right. Scarling. Yes." He nodded vigorously. "It'll stay by the studio. It hates the Mandolinis for imprisoning it."

Serena put her hands on her hips. "Whoever invented that thing was *stupid*," she said angrily. "Why would you make an awful little monster that could drain illuminations?"

"Tybalt didn't always think things through..." said Payne absently. "Do you think it would like to meet the spoons?"

Tybalt?

Wait, does he mean...?

"Payne," said Rosa, in a very calm, very even voice that sounded like her grandmother when she was very, very angry, "did you mean just now that *Tybalt* was the one who made the Scarling?"

Payne jerked his head up guiltily. "I—uh—oh. Uh. Did I not mention that?"

"Tybalt Mandolini?"

Payne became very interested in grooming the feathers under his wing.

"You did *not* mention that!" Rosa snatched up the barrette, furious. "You said he made enemies!"

"I didn't lie," Payne mumbled into his wing. "He made the Scarling, and it *was* his enemy."

"You know that wasn't what I thought! You let me think somebody made it to get back at him!"

"Well, the Scarling *does* want to get back at him," Payne said. "And, uh...it doesn't really like me very much, either."

"At the moment, *I* don't like you very much, Payne!" snapped Rosa. "You lied to me!"

"I didn't lie!" said Payne. "I just...um...didn't mention some of the details. They didn't matter. You didn't need to know! We had to catch the Scarling anyway! And Tybalt was a good master, and he was my friend, and if you knew that he made the Scarling, you'd think it was *his* fault—look, Tybalt was a good person!" He hopped back and forth on his feet, clearly upset. "He *was!* It wasn't his fault the Scarling went bad!"

He looked from Serena to Rosa and back again, in anguish. "He was my family," he croaked.

A light came on. "Rosa, Serena, go to bed!" shouted Grandmama. "Don't think I can't hear you chattering in there!"

They sat in silence. Rosa fumed. She couldn't believe that after she'd kept Payne's secret and gotten in trouble for it that the crow hadn't told her the truth.

Then he drew me with the charcoal, Payne had said. It was Tybalt who had used the Scarling's charcoal. Not to make monsters, but to make Payne himself.

The longer she thought about it, the madder she got. She'd been keeping so many secrets and running herself ragged while Payne was lying to protect someone who had been dead for two hundred years.

Because Tybalt had been his family.

Well, Rosa had a family, too.

Rosa got up. She pulled her blanket around her shoulders. She walked to Uncle Alfonso's bay, ignoring Serena's question behind her.

"Uncle?" she whispered. "Are you still awake?"

She heard the movement as he sat up. "Yes, Rosalita. What is it?"

"I've got something I need to tell you..."

TWENTY-SEVEN

Night
Blackberry Day
Thermidor, the Month of Heat

IT SOUNDED CRAZY. It sounded like make-believe. She didn't know if she could have told anyone but Uncle Alfonso, who always listened to her.

"...and the crow came off the box..."

Halfway through she started crying and Uncle Alfonso handed her a tissue.

"I wanted to tell you," said Rosa, hiccuping. "I *did!*"

"You told me now," said Uncle Alfonso, taking her small hand in between his large ones. "That's the important thing. Now we can fix it."

"So you believe me?"

"I believe you."

"Tell us what?" said Grandmama.

The question hung like a drop of paint on the end of a paintbrush, suspended in time. Rosa stared down at her bandaged hand, which itched where the Scarling had bit her. Could you get a horrible disease from being bit by an enchanted mandrake root? *Probably. My hand will probably fall off. Given how everything else is going.*

"Rosa?" said Uncle Alfonso. They had all gathered in Aunt Nadia's bay, so that the angel painting did not go unprotected.

Rosa looked around for Payne. The crow was perched on the wall of the bay, his beak open in distress.

"I know what's making the drawings," she confessed. "I tried to stop it by myself, but I can't. And the crow's part of it, and I thought he was my friend but he lied to me."

Payne's wings drooped at her words. Then everyone turned to stare at him and he straightened up again and pretended to ignore them.

Rosa hoped that he would say something, but he didn't. *Fine.* She looked around at her family's puzzled faces and swallowed. If she had to do this herself, she would. "It started about two hundred years ago with an artist named Tybalt Mandolini..."

She was only a few sentences in when Sergio said, "Tybalt!" and charged from the bay.

Rosa paused, looking after him. "Keep talking!" he called, accompanied by the sounds of rummaging. "Hear you!"

Rosa explained what she'd pieced together about Tybalt making the Scarling and later Payne. She'd just gotten to the bit where she'd opened the box and released the Scarling when Sergio reappeared, holding a thick book.

"Tybalt!" he said, slamming the book down on Aunt Nadia's desk. "Artist!"

They all crowded around, studying the book. It was an art history book, and there were three large color plates under the heading, *Mandolini, Tybalt.*

"Not bad technique," Nadia said. "Composition's a bit stiff."

"That was the style back then," said Uncle Marco. "Good use of color, I'd say."

Grandmama put her hands on her hips. "He made an evil monster that's out to ruin us! Does it really matter how good his technique was?"

"Of course it matters," said Aunt Nadia with a half-smile. "You'd hate to see the studio destroyed by a *mediocre* artist, wouldn't you?"

Grandmama snorted. Serena giggled. Uncle Marco turned a page. "Let's see...trained under Royal...married in 1652... buried under the Great Cathedral in 1679..."

"What!?" squawked a voice from overhead.

Everyone froze, then very slowly turned to look up at Payne.

The crow dropped to the desk. Nadia took a step back. Uncle Marco stood quite still, his hand on the page, and murmured something. The only word that Rosa could catch was "interesting."

Payne stared at the page very hard, first with one eye, then the other. "1679," he said. "Thirty-five years after I went on the box! He had thirty-five *years!*"

"Talks!" said Cousin Sergio, in a carrying whisper.

The crow shook himself all over, as if trying to get water droplets off his wings, then turned to Rosa. "You're right," he said. He took a deep breath. "I'm sorry. I should have told you everything."

"I WISH someone would tell *me* everything," said Grandmama, in the silence that followed.

Payne hopped down to the floor, turned, and bowed to the old woman with his wings spread. Grandmama's eyebrows went up so high that they nearly touched her hair.

"This is my fault," said Payne. "I was the one who told her to keep silent. But I think now we've come to a time when silence will not save us."

Rosa could have thrown her arms around the bird and kissed his beak.

"I need more coffee if I'm going to deal with this," said Aunt Nadia, and headed toward the kitchen.

"Master Crow," said Uncle Alfonso, bowing slightly to Payne, "I believe that would be a very good idea. Let us all have coffee or hot chocolate, and then you—and Rosa—can explain everything."

Payne nodded. "I'll do my best," he said. He fluttered up to Rosa's shoulder and draped his wing across the back of her neck. "I'm sorry," he said again, in her ear.

They all went into the kitchen, to the long table. Aunt Nadia and Sergio lugged the angel painting into the hallway, because Nadia refused to miss the explanation or leave her painting unguarded, and Grandmama refused to go without tea. When she discovered that there were only two spoons left, there was a great deal of confused muttering.

"Payne—" Rosa began.

"So, about the Scarling!" Payne said hurriedly.

He did most of the talking. Rosa interjected where she could. The kitchen was quiet except for the harsh sound of the crow's voice, and the sound of seven people listening intently.

"Extraordinary," said Uncle Marco when he had finished.

"But do you have any proof?" asked Aunt Nadia skeptically.

"Madam," said Payne, with dignity, "I *am* proof."

"You're a *crow*," said Aunt Nadia. "It's very impressive that you're a talking crow, but it doesn't prove that anything else is going on. And no offense intended, but how do we know you aren't responsible yourself? No one has seen any of these things except you and Rosa, and things started to go badly when you showed up."

Rosa's mouth fell open. "But he wouldn't—he's *not*—"

He lied to you once already, whispered the little voice in her head.

Serena cleared her throat.

She'd been very quiet the entire time, but now she held up the jar that held the scribbling.

The scribbling still lay at the bottom of the glass. As they watched, it banged its crayon aimlessly against the side of the jar.

"I put the lid back on while everyone was yelling," said Serena, and even though she sounded a little snotty saying it, Rosa wanted to cheer. "This thing was in our studio. It attacked *my* illuminations."

Uncle Marco took the jar and gazed at it for a few moments. "Interesting. *Very* interesting."

"Front door!" said Sergio abruptly. "Just like it!"

"Yes..." Nadia took the jar and turned it. "Yes, it does look like it, doesn't it?" She inclined her head toward Payne. "An argument in your favor, Master Crow, if this is indeed the drawing from the door."

Payne nodded. "You're wise to ask for proof," he said. "It all sounds quite mad, I realize. Even for people who are used to illuminations."

"Creating life," said Uncle Alfonso. "It does sound like the stuff of fairy tales."

"It wasn't easy," Payne said. "Tybalt didn't believe in it either, until he literally stumbled across the technique and started experimenting. It takes a particular magical talent and in the end, he could only use his gift to create the Scarling. But with its charcoal, he could create so much more."

Uncle Marco nodded. "He used his skills to make a tool, and the right tool made everything easier. Like using a knife to cut a tree to make an axe handle. Once you have the axe, it's much easier to cut the next hundred trees."

"The opposite of what poor Francis tried," murmured Uncle Alfonso.

Payne hopped onto the kitchen table and tapped the charcoal. "Without this, its power is very much less."

Uncle Alfonso took the charcoal and studied it. "Vine charcoal," he said. "Made the real old-fashioned way. But so dense." He tapped the stick against the table and it did not break. "A regular piece snaps in half if you look at it funny."

"It was made from the Scarling's own taproot," said Payne. "The last mandrake root to leave the soil. It never runs down."

"It doesn't feel wicked," said Uncle Alfonso thoughtfully. "A bit like an illumination, but not a bad one. Here, Marco, feel."

Uncle Marco took it and rubbed his fingers over the stick,

leaving black smudges. "Hmm. You're right. It doesn't feel malicious."

"Do bad illuminations feel bad?" asked Rosa. She'd never seen one.

Uncle Alfonso shook his head. "Most of them just feel like magic. *You* know, Rosalita." Rosa nodded, thinking of the fuzzy animal-hair feeling of the paintings in the Tax Office. "There are wicked ones that are only there to hurt people. Those feel...nasty. When that apprentice was trying to hurt me...well." He shook his head sadly. "They felt like...like holding a jar with a wasp buzzing in it. A very angry vibration. But an illumination often isn't good or bad by itself. It's like a knife. You could use it to cut canvas or to stab someone."

"There will be no stabbing at my dinner table!" said Grandmama. She took the charcoal herself. "Hmm. I don't feel anything. Then again, I was never much of an illuminator."

Payne shrugged. "It's not inherently bad. The Scarling wasn't either, but it *went* bad."

"People do sometimes, too," said Uncle Marco.

"Why'd it go bad?" asked Serena, placing the box on the table.

Payne looked embarrassed. "Well...you know how these things are..."

He sounded a bit like he did when admitting to taking the spoons. Rosa turned her head and gave him a very stern look. "Payne."

"Fine," muttered Payne. "You sound just like him, you know, when you use that tone of voice."

"Him who?"

"Tybalt Mandolini." He lowered his wing. "Tybalt made us both. He made the Scarling first, though, on the mandrake root.

It was...um. Limited. It couldn't talk. Then he made me. I was made of paint, but he put feathers into it. The paint was very thick, you understand."

"Impasto technique," said Uncle Marco, nodding. "Very thick brush strokes to give the painting life. There are some where the paint's an inch or more thick, and you can embed things in the layers."

"Exactly," said Payne, nodding. "He was good at it. Always adding little bits here and there. I was his masterpiece."

He said it with pride, raising his head and spreading out his wings. For a moment he looked more like a falcon than a crow.

Rosa looked at him admiringly—and saw Serena, on the other side of his wings.

The Scarling doesn't like me, Payne had said.

And she remembered how she'd felt, when Serena got a commission, and her stomach twisted just a little at the memory.

"The Scarling got jealous, didn't it?" she said quietly. "That's why it hates you. It wasn't that you helped trap it. It was that Tybalt liked you best."

The whole family looked at her. Uncle Alfonso reached out and squeezed her shoulder.

Payne's wings sagged. "Once he created me, he paid less attention to the Scarling. It had been his chief assistant, you understand." He landed on the painted box and scuffed a claw over the hinges. "But it was his first and clumsiest creation, and since Tybalt had the gift, he eventually found that he didn't need the Scarling to sketch for him to make more. He could just use its charcoal. And I can see, sometimes, what an illumination needs to work better, which is useful. So Tybalt forgot the Scarling unless he needed it, and it got...angry."

Rosa felt conflicted. She could almost feel sorry for the Scarling, cast aside by its creator. But it had ruined so many things, and tried to ruin Aunt Nadia's great painting, and made the scribblings that had ruined so many more.

"Tybalt probably shouldn't have ignored it," said Rosa.

"No," said Payne. "He wasn't a bad man, you understand. He wasn't *trying* to make anyone wicked. But Tybalt was single-minded when he worked, and once he learned a technique, he didn't really care about it any more. He'd be obsessed with learning it, with making it better, and then he'd just abandon it as soon as he was done."

Uncle Marco snorted. "I don't know *anyone* like that," Sergio, who would dedicate a year to mastering a technique, and then drop it as soon as it no longer interested him, gave an embarrassed cough.

Payne looked briefly amused, but the expression faded. "He was like that with people too, I'm afraid. He'd be your dearest friend for a week, and then he'd forget you existed. People didn't take that well. Neither did the Scarling. Just like he forgot I existed once I went on the box. It was only supposed to be a few months. Just until he figured out how to unmake it without unmaking everything he used its charcoal to create."

"Like you," said Rosa.

"Like me," admitted Payne. "But I've been a fool. I assumed that something must have happened to him right afterward. But he lived for thirty-five more years!" Rosa could see the fine down around his beak trembling. "He forgot me, too. When he couldn't do it right away, he got caught up in something else and probably put the box somewhere and told himself he'd get back to it in a few days. But the day never came and he died and I've been trying to protect the memory of someone who forgot I *existed*."

He turned his head and shoved his beak into Rosa's hair, clearly distressed. Rosa leaned her cheek against the crow's side. She was still a little mad, but Payne was so obviously hurt that she decided to save being mad for later. She picked up the charcoal on the table and began doodling a radish on her napkin to give the crow time to recover his composure.

It was quiet in the kitchen. Grandmama got up and made more coffee.

"Well," said Uncle Alfonso. "He was a Mandolini, and I wish I could say that any of that surprises me, but we have always been easily fascinated and even more easily distracted. And occasionally too talented for our own good."

Payne sighed and extracted himself from Rosa's collar. "I *must* stop the Scarling," he said. "Rosa got its charcoal away, but it can still make mischief. And it won't fall for the same trap twice."

"So what do you suggest?" asked Uncle Marco.

"You mean you'll help me?" asked Payne.

"Of course we will," said Grandmama. "The blasted thing is destroying my kitchen and drawing on my walls! Did you think we'd just wash our hands of it and say you're on your own?"

"Well," said Payne, glancing guiltily at Rosa. "I did make Rosa keep silent. That was a mistake. I thought...well, never mind. But you should know, she kept saying we should tell you. This isn't her fault."

"Rosa's a good girl," said Uncle Alfonso firmly. "And will be a fine artist some day."

"Yes, yes!" said Cousin Sergio impatiently. "But! Monsters! What now?"

"The important thing is that now we've got the charcoal," Payne said. "It can't feed without it. Probably." He flipped the latch on the box open with his bill. "So now we just put the charcoal in here and then we have to keep this box under lock and key, until it is so weakened that we can catch it easily."

"Won't it try to get the charcoal back?" asked Aunt Nadia. "I would, if I were it."

"Probably," admitted Payne. "But it's not that strong by itself."

"Except that it's not by itself," said Serena slowly. "It's got an entire army of scribbly things, doesn't it?"

Payne's beak fell open.

After a moment, the crow said "I'd almost forgotten about them. Well. Yes, I suppose. But they won't last long without the Scarling feeding them power."

"They ruined my illuminations!" said Serena.

"Whole studio full! Lot of damage!" put in Cousin Sergio.

"And they drew on some of the illuminations next door," said Rosa. "I've been drawing radishes to ward them off for *days*."

"It would seem," said Uncle Alfonso, "that we should prepare to be under siege. However long it takes for a—scribbling, was it?—to fade away if it isn't fed."

"That would probably be best," said Payne.

"I'll get Walter," said Uncle Marco. "This is a bad time for him to go wandering."

"It's a shame we can't make our own scribblings," said Aunt Nadia. "An army to fight an army!"

Payne gave her an approving look. "I wish we could. Tybalt

could have. But that's a rare gift, even in a family of illuminators."

"Maybe not so rare," said Grandmama quietly.

There was something about her voice, even softly, that
made everyone look at her.

She pointed.

On the table, Rosa's napkin lay forgotten. The charcoal
drawing of the fanged radish was there, and it was...

Moving.

"Whoa!" said Cousin Sergio.

"My goodness!" said Uncle Marco.

As they watched, the radish set its leaves and pushed itself
off the paper. The lines were thick and clear. The scribbles that
Rosa had made to test the charcoal formed a rough halo over its
head, like a tiny vegetable angel.

It shook itself, wiped its fangs with its leaves, and looked
around.

Then it waddled toward Rosa, who drew back in surprise.

It sat down in front of her, and looked up at her. It was hard
to tell, in a mostly transparent creature made of lines, but it
looked...hopeful.

Rosa swallowed hard, and reached out a finger.

She stroked the drawn leaves. They felt coarse, like pastel
paper, and a faint black smudge appeared on her fingers again.

The radish chirped. It sounded like a cross between a bird
and the squeak of a pencil on smooth paper.

"Oh my," said Grandmama, and Rosa looked up to see her
entire family gazing at her with awe in their faces.

TWENTY-EIGHT

"This is impossible," said Payne.

He'd said this about twenty times already, and Rosa was getting a bit tired of it.

"Tybalt was special," said the crow. "No other illuminators had his gift. You can't have done it!"

He looked around the kitchen as if expecting to find Tybalt hiding somewhere in the corner.

The fanged radish scribbling had curled up in the crook of Rosa's elbow and appeared to have gone to sleep. It weighed nothing, but Rosa could feel the faintest pressure, like a breath against her arm.

"Not impossible!" said Cousin Sergio. "Improbable!"

Everyone looked at him. Sergio spread his hands and made an effort to talk more slowly. "It happened!" he said. "Can't be impossible if it happened!" He took a deep breath. "So just— very unlikely!"

"Well," said Grandmama, "I suppose that's true."

"What are the odds, really?" asked Aunt Nadia. "That Rosa—who's a great kid and will be a fine illuminator, don't get me wrong—would have a talent like that?" She folded her hands around her coffee cup. "*And,* as you say, that the radishes she's been drawing since she was in diapers would be the illumination that defended against these little scribbly beasts?"

"But they *aren't* illuminations," said Rosa. This was the most frustrating thing for her. She knew more about the radishes than anyone else, and she knew that they weren't real illuminations. "You've all seen them, you know...they aren't *magic.*"

Uncle Alfonso nodded. "Art is its own kind of magic, Rosalita, and they were wonderful." He smiled. "But more practically, no, they weren't *quite* illuminations."

"They were close," said Payne. "I felt it. Like a door that's open just a crack."

"Our feathered friend here is correct," said Uncle Marco. "There was always a little magic to Rosa's radishes. I had thought that it was just that Rosa herself had a powerful potential gift for illumination, and it was spilling over...but perhaps it's more than that." He tapped his fingers on the table. "She was the one who found the box, too. No, I do not think it is a matter of odds."

A powerful potential gift? Me?

"If you put two illuminators in a city that has none, they will run into each other on a street corner before the week is out," Uncle Marco said. "Depend upon it. Magic calls to magic."

"That's true," said Uncle Alfonso. "Why, once when I was traveling to Prague—well, never mind, the details aren't important."

"You think the box called me?" Rosa found that she didn't particularly like the idea that she'd been digging around in the basement because the box had wanted her to do so. *I was bored, and I did it because I wanted to...didn't I?*

She remembered her suggestion, days earlier, that there might be an illumination might make people like art. Suddenly it seemed much more dangerous. *You wouldn't ever know if you liked a painting or if the magic forced you to do it. You wouldn't know if you liked anything or if there was magic in your head.* She shuddered at the thought.

Uncle Alfonso was watching her and drew her into a hug. "Don't fret, Rosalita. It is also possible that your magic drew the box to you, not the other way around. After all, it's been in the basement for two hundreds years, and none of us were drawn to it. I suspect that your radish drawings may have been the key."

"But I've drawn dozens of radishes!" said Rosa. "And none of them were real illuminations!"

"Hundreds!" countered Cousin Sergio.

"It's the halo," said Serena abruptly.

There was a brief pause. Rosa looked down at the radish in her arms and her mouth fell open.

"You never drew them with a halo before," Serena said impatiently. "That's got to be it."

"Eh?" said Cousin Sergio.

"No..." said Rosa, remembering days spent lying on her stomach on the floor of Serena's room, drawing radishes with wings, radishes breathing fire, radishes riding horses...but never haloes. "No, I never did."

"Are you certain?" asked Grandmama.

Serena shared a frustrated look with Rosa. Grown-ups could be very slow on the uptake. "Positive," she said.

Uncle Alfonso came to their rescue. "The smallest change can matter, with an illumination. You all know that. Rosa, draw another one. Don't put a halo on it."

Rosa felt very self-conscious as she drew another radish with the charcoal. "I can't do this when you all stare at me," she mumbled.

Everyone looked away hurriedly, which was almost worse. Exasperated, Grandmama said "If you're all going to be in the kitchen anyway, we can start on the dishes."

There were general groans. Aunt Nadia ran out to go check on her painting again. Rosa bent over the napkin again, while the sounds of scrubbing and drying and banging filled the kitchen behind her.

Payne picked up Aunt Nadia's coffee spoon and began casually strolling toward the door. Grandmama put her hand down and snapped her fingers at him.

"Buh ish shinee," mumbled the crow around the handle of the spoon.

"And it's very nearly the last spoon in the house," said Grandmama, "and I'm getting a little suspicious about that."

"You said that Tybalt put real crow feathers in your paint?" asked Uncle Marco. "I suspect I know where the love of shiny things came from."

Payne surrendered the spoon and became suddenly very interested in something under his wing.

Rosa's radish drawing woke up and hopped onto her shoulder, looking interested. She didn't mind him.

She finished the drawing and set the charcoal down.

When the dishes were done, everyone came crowding around and looked down at the napkin.

Uncle Marco laid a finger delicately over the drawing. "Yes," he said. "You can feel it. It's got magic, but it's not...not *live*. Not an illumination."

Aunt Nadia tapped a nail on the napkin and nodded. "He's right," she said. "It's like when you start a painting, and you've just got the first strokes in. You can feel that it will be one, but it isn't there yet."

"Now draw in a halo if you would, Rosalita," said Uncle Alfonso.

Rosa gulped. She was suddenly afraid that it wouldn't work. She glanced up at Serena.

Her friend smiled at her, and for a minute it was like they were both younger and in Serena's room, talking about what they were drawing. "It'll work," said Serena. "I know it will."

With a hand that only shook a little, Rosa drew a wobbly halo around the radish's head, or what passed for a head on a root vegetable.

For a long moment, nothing happened. Aunt Nadia reached toward the napkin, frowning.

Her fingers hadn't quite touched it when the radish began to wiggle. Nadia snatched her hand back, and a rare grin spread across her narrow face.

It stretched. The first radish, on Rosa's shoulder, made a chirp of delight.

The new radish seemed to hear the sound. It pulled itself up off the paper and looked around. When it saw the other one (and how it saw without eyes, Rosa had no idea) it let out a chirp of its own and began to climb up Rosa's arm.

The two living drawings settled in on Rosa's shoulder,

looking for all the world like a pair of birds cuddled together. They cooed softly to one another, and one flipped its leaves over the other like a hug.

"Told you it was the halo," said Serena, looking smug.

"This is impossible—" began Payne.

"Impossible or not," said Uncle Alfonso, "it's true. Your Tybalt could do it, and it seems our Rosa can, too."

TWENTY-NINE

GRANDMAMA HAD MADE up another pot of coffee for the adults and more hot chocolate for the two kids. Rosa had gone back to her room, careful not to disturb the radishes, and rescued three more spoons from under her bed.

"Was this your doing, Payne?" asked Grandmama.

"Certainly not," said Payne, without much conviction. "They...um...must have migrated there. On their own."

Grandmama folded her arms and tapped her foot.

"Spoons like to be with other spoons," said Payne. "They feel more comfortable in a herd."

Grandmama gave him a long, level look, which Rosa recognized. She was just glad it wasn't directed at her.

"At any rate," said the crow hurriedly, "we've got more important matters to attend to. The Scarling will come back for the charcoal." He puffed out his throat feathers. "It'll have to, in order to feed. If we don't want to be fending off scribblings, that's when we'll have our chance to catch it."

"Should we make another trap like we did before? Wouldn't it recognize it this time?" asked Rosa. She couldn't imagine that the Scarling would fall for that twice.

Payne seemed to agree. He shook his head. "The Scarling's too smart for that. If we set a trap, it'll have to be totally different—and better hidden."

There was a long pause, and then everyone began talking at once.

"Dig a hole!" barked Cousin Sergio. "Scarling falls in! Boom!"

"Perhaps we could bait a trap with something it likes to eat?" said Grandmama.

"Cover the walls in illuminations," said Uncle Marco. "Drive it out of hiding!"

"Let's just tear the building down," said Aunt Nadia.

Her suggestion fell into one of those breaks when everyone else has finished speaking. Everyone stared at her.

She took a long swallow of coffee. "What? It'd take care of the problem."

"You are not tearing down the studio!" said Grandmama. "Really, Nadia! That's your solution to everything!"

Aunt Nadia gazed down into her coffee cup. "And yet you never let me actually do it."

Serena's eyes were as round as saucers.

"Don't worry," Rosa whispered, leaning over. "She'd never really do it. Probably."

Uncle Alfonso winked at them. "Nadia never was willing to fix anything. If she made a mistake, she'd rather throw it away and start fresh than paint over it."

"I heard that," said Aunt Nadia. "And I am fixing my

glorious painting of angels that this Scarling ruined, I'll have you know."

"Only because you can't bear the thought of re-painting all those folds of fabric," said Grandmama. She refilled Nadia's coffee cup.

"Which reminds me," said Aunt Nadia, standing up, "I should go and watch over it. Do let me know what you all decide to do." Over her shoulder, she added, "Or if I need to get the sledgehammer."

After she left, everyone stared at the table. Rosa carefully adjusted the radishes on her shoulder.

"Your aunt is so *cool*," whispered Serena.

"Well, *yeah*," whispered Rosa back. "If you didn't always want to draw at your house, you'd have found that out sooner!"

"My bedroom's nicer."

"Girls..." said Grandmama.

"Right," said Serena hurriedly. "Could we search the studio? See if we can find the Scarling?"

"Not the basements," said Uncle Alfonso. "A small crea-ture could hide anywhere down there. There's three hundred years of accumulated junk."

"Some of it's quite valuable," said Grandmama defensively. "Probably. I keep meaning to go through it."

"It wouldn't help," said Uncle Marco. "There's enough taxidermy in this place alone for a whole army to hide in. All they'd have to do is make a little hole and climb inside. We'd think it was moths and walk right past it."

Cousin Sergio looked horrified. He'd finished his mermaid commission some days ago, and was currently working on one that involved two stuffed flamingos and a moth-eaten lynx. "Be back! Got to check!" he cried, and ran out the door.

In the end, it was Grandmama who determined the next course of action. "It's after midnight," she said. "Everybody go to bed. We'll figure out what to do in the morning."

"How do we guard the charcoal, though?" asked Rosa. She set the charcoal into the box and closed it, but the latch seemed very flimsy.

"I'll guard it," said Payne. He perched on top of the lid.

Uncle Marco looked at him thoughtfully, then said, "That's a good idea. But let's try and be even safer."

He limped from the kitchen and returned a few minutes later with a length of chain and Cousin Sergio.

"Was painting that! Not done!"

"You painted it two days ago," said Uncle Marco. "Now you're just fiddling with the highlights. Work on the flamingos, they need it more."

Cousin Sergio muttered under his breath, but helped Marco to wrap the chain around the crow box. It was very heavy and had links as thick as Rosa's thumb.

"There's no lock for it," said Grandmama.

"No, but if you were a few inches tall, you'd probably have a hard time moving it," said Uncle Marco reasonably.

Payne nodded. "A good thought," he said. He perched atop the box again, gripping the links with his claws. "We should polish it," he said. "Make it nice and shiny."

"In which case you'd stuff it under poor Rosa's bed," said Grandmama severely. Payne muttered something, sounding remarkably like Cousin Sergio for a moment.

Rosa carefully lifted the two radishes down from her shoulder. "Help Payne guard the box," she told them.

They chirped. She wondered if they understood what she was saying. Still, the scribblings really hadn't liked the radish drawings, so hopefully they wouldn't like the live radishes any more.

Are my radishes scribblings?

Rosa chewed her lower lip as she and Serena went slowly back to her bay. She didn't like to think of her radishes as scribblings. The scribblings had wreaked too much havoc in the studio.

Serena yawned as they climbed into bed. "Well," she said. "That didn't go quite the way we expected, did it?"

"No," said Rosa. "But I'm glad it all came out." She was tired, but more than that, she was relieved. She felt as if she had just taken off shoes that were too tight and could finally relax.

But she also didn't want to forget Serena's role. "You helped," she said. "You mostly believed me when I couldn't tell anybody else. Thanks."

In the dark, she felt Serena shrug. "Eh," she said. "We're friends. And I'd have to be pretty stupid not to believe *something* was going on, after that thing got into my gryphons."

Rosa grinned, even though she knew Serena couldn't see her. From anybody else, that might have been a grudging admission. From Serena, it was a shout of confidence.

And we're friends again. And that's the important thing.

There was one more thing she needed to confess. She took a deep breath. "I was jealous of your commission at first," she whispered. "Really jealous."

Serena sighed. "I wanted you to be. But that was before I realized how boring drawing a hundred gryphons would be." She was silent for a moment, then added, "That's probably why my dad told me that illuminators shouldn't be jealous of each other. He's probably had to draw a *million* gryphons."

Rosa giggled, thinking of how many times her uncle had to draw Walter.

"You girls go to bed now!" called Grandmama. "No more giggling or talking about boys or whatever it is you do!"

"Boys!" muttered Serena. "That's just what we don't need."

"I thought you liked boys," whispered Rosa.

"To *look* at. Not to do *important* stuff."

"I mean it!" shouted Grandmama, and they went to sleep and hardly giggled at all.

THIRTY

Very Early Morning
Watering Day
Thermidor, the Month of Heat

ROSA AWOKE to a tremendous crash from the kitchen.

She thought immediately of the Scarling and Payne. *Payne!*
Was he okay?

She was halfway out of the bay before she realized she was
even out of bed. Her bare feet slapped on the cold tile floor.

"Eh?" said Serena, sitting up groggily. "What was that?"
but Rosa was already gone.

She heard running footsteps behind her. Aunt Nadia's bay
was closest to the kitchen and she and Rosa hit the doorway at
the same time.

It was so late that it was actually early. The little window over the sink let in the cold gray glow of pre-dawn.

The crow box was on the floor. "Caw!" shouted Payne from the far doorway. "Caw caw *caw!*"

On top of the box was the Scarling.

"Gah!" said Aunt Nadia, and Rosa remembered that she'd never seen it before.

The Scarling looked up at them and bared its painted teeth. It was hauling on the chains around the box.

One of Rosa's radishes was trying to reach the box, but a circle of scribblings were trying to drive it away. As she watched, it struck out with its leaves and its enemies scattered, only to tighten the circle again a moment later.

Clank! The Scarling shoved a loop of chain free.

"Pardon, Rosa," said Aunt Nadia, sounding as dry and calm as ever, and pushed past her. She took two running steps—and *kicked* the Scarling off the box as if it were a ball.

Thud. The Scarling flew in an arc across the kitchen, hit the cupboards, and slid off.

Rosa leapt forward and threw herself belly-down over the box. The wooden edges dug into her ribs, but nobody was getting into it without going through her first.

"Caw!" shouted Payne from the doorway. "Caw! Get off me, you little—*raaaawk!*"

Scribblings converged on Rosa. Rosa felt them jabbing at her skin, like dozens of sharpened pencil points. "Ow! Ow!"

The Scarling came groggily to its feet, swayed, then sat down again. The painted face looked confused.

Rosa didn't see much more, because a scribbling leapt on her face. Rosa yelped and swatted at it, but that meant that she had to lift an arm away from the box. Immediately she felt the box sliding away as the scribblings converged on it and began to pull.

She batted her attacker off her face and clutched for the box again, sweeping the scribblings aside with her elbow. They weighed nothing, but she felt as if she were waving her arm through a swarm of hornets. Little lines jabbed at her like sharp pencil points. "Owww!"

"Rosa!"

Before she could respond, she found herself being hauled backward across the kitchen floor by the ankles.

The loose end of the chain clattered against the kitchen tiles—*clank clank clank!*

The arm that the scribblings had stung wasn't working properly somehow. When she tried to wrap it around the box, it took much too long to respond and her fingers seemed thick and swollen.

She actually recognized the scribbling that went for her face next. It was the very first one she'd seen on the wall, the one she'd been blamed for drawing and hadn't been able to clean up.

Its nasty grin had gotten larger and nastier. Its teeth glittered paper-bright. It opened its mouth and Rosa saw the inside of its jaws, shaded with charcoal.

She squeezed her eyes shut.

There was a soft *swish* sound, as if someone had flipped through a pad of paper, and Rosa felt a breath of movement against her skin.

She opened her eyes.

Her other radish was on her shoulder. It had slapped her attacker aside with its tail. The grinning scribbling was trying to retreat, but the radish leapt down and landed on top of the enemy scribbling, hard.

Charcoal dust puffed into the air.

Whoever had hold of Rosa's ankles gave another yank. Rosa was pulled right out of the kitchen, dragging the box and chain behind her.

And then Cousin Sergio was picking her up in his arms, out of reach of the scribblings. "Rosa!" he barked. "Hurt? I'll kill 'em!"

"The box!" gasped Rosa. She threw her good arm around his neck so that the box was pressed between them.

"CAW!" Rosa saw Payne soar across the kitchen. Aunt Nadia stood behind him, her hair in disarray and her hands covered in charcoal dust. The second radish was perched on her shoulder like an odd little bird.

The Scarling made a small, nasty sound, like nails scratching on wood, and fled behind a cupboard.

The scribblings ran after it. In a few seconds, there was no one left in the kitchen but Payne, Nadia, Cousin Sergio and Rosa and her radishes.

The entire encounter had taken less than a minute.

Very slowly, Cousin Sergio let Rosa down. Rosa clutched the box, one-handed. Payne landed on the table, looking at Rosa. The skin around his eyes and beak had gone very pale.

"Nadia? Sergio? What happened?" asked Grandmama from the hallway.

"Our nasty little friend went for the box," said Aunt Nadia. She began making coffee. She was limping a little, and Rosa could see bright red welts along her ankles.

Payne hung his head. "It set a trap for me," he admitted. "And I fell into it like a chick just out of the egg."

"What do you mean?" asked Grandmama.

Shamefaced, Payne hopped along the floor to the doorway, and picked up a fallen object on the floor.

He held it up. The first light of sunrise through the window gleamed off a perfectly ordinary, everyday spoon.

THIRTY-ONE

Morning
Watering Day
Thermidor, the Month of Heat

"Oh, PAYNE," said Rosa.

"The scribblings must have dragged it into the hall," the crow admitted. "And then they waited for it to get light enough for me to see it. I never heard them move. And I saw it, and... well...I thought that someone must have dropped it last night, and I'd just go for an instant, you understand, and the radishes were on guard, so it wouldn't matter..."

His head sank down as he spoke and his feathers were fluffed up in all directions where the scribblings had jumped on him. He looked so miserable that Rosa wanted to hug him, even though she mostly wanted to yell at him.

"The important thing," said Aunt Nadia, with remarkable calm, "is that that—*thing*—didn't get the charcoal." She inclined her head to Payne. "And I owe you an apology, Master Crow. Now that I've actually seen that Scarling creature..." She trailed off, shaking her head.

Rosa felt that Aunt Nadia was selling herself far too short. "*Seen* it!?" she cried. "You kicked it! It was amazing!"

Nadia suppressed a smile as she looked into her empty coffee cup. "Well," she said. "One never *quite* knows what one will do in a moment of panic."

Cousin Sergio was still hovering worriedly over Rosa. "Heard yelling! Tried to help!"

"I hope I didn't kick you," said Rosa. "They were stinging me and I was afraid I'd drop the box."

"What in the name of the saints is wrong with your *arm?!*" cried Grandmama.

Rosa set the box down on the table. Payne leapt on top of it, and the two radishes took up positions on either side.

Her arm was swelling the same way that Nadia's ankles were. It was hard to bend her elbow, and there were welts up and down it as if she'd been bitten by bugs.

Each welt was a little red spot surrounded by a hard circle. In the center of the red spot was a black dot, exactly as if she'd been stabbed with a pencil and had some strange allergic reaction to it.

"The scribblings got me," said Rosa. She told herself she wasn't going to cry.

Aunt Nadia sat down heavily and put her swollen foot up on the chair. "Me too. But I think Rosa got it worse."

Grandmama's scowl would have put any cathedral gargoyle

to shame, but her fingers were gentle as she took Rosa's arm. "Does it still hurt?"

"A little," said Rosa. "But not like a bee-sting. More like a mosquito bite. It itches a bit."

"Well, don't scratch." She leveled a grim look at Payne. "Well, crow? Do you know anything about this?"

Payne drooped even more. "Tybalt got stabbed by scribblings while he was locking up the Scarling, but he painted me onto the box right away, so I didn't see how he treated it. I'm sorry. This is all my fault!"

Grandmama stomped into the pantry and came back with a jar of honey. "We'll treat it as if it's a bug bite," she said, and went off to the balcony to pull leaves from one of her potted plants.

"Angry!" said Cousin Sergio.

"Just a bit," said Aunt Nadia dryly. "Sergio, pour me some coffee, will you?"

"Can't! Not ready!"

Payne crept toward Rosa. "I'm sorry," he said again. "Rosa, I didn't realize—I'd forgotten they could do that—"

"It's all right," said Rosa mechanically. She hated to see anyone so upset, even if she knew that she had every right to be mad at the crow. But being mad didn't seem like it would help much. She had other concerns right now. "Do you think I'm going to die?"

"You won't!" said Payne. "I mean—you—no, you *couldn't*—"

Rosa stared at her arm. Her mouth felt dry.

"Tybalt probably didn't die of scribbling stings, then," said Aunt Nadia, "if he made it thirty-five years after. But somebody should still probably look that up."

A tear leaked down Rosa's face.

"No!" said Cousin Sergio. "Don't cry!" He looked as if he might cry himself. "Saved box! Very brave!"

"I refuse to die until I've had coffee," said Aunt Nadia. "I won't do it." She leaned over the table and tapped Rosa's cheek with her finger. "I'd hold out for some hot chocolate, if I were you." Rosa managed a weak smile.

"No one is dying," said Grandmama angrily. She bustled back into the room, holding flat green leaves. "Sergio, stop lurking around and go find me some of those new bandages with an illumination for healing on them." She paused and rolled her eyes. "Assuming the accursed things haven't gotten into those, too."

"There'll be some at my house," volunteered Serena. Rosa wondered how long she'd been there. She wiped her face with her free hand. She didn't want Serena to see her crying.

"I'd be grateful if you could run and fetch two," said Grandmama. "Give my regards to your mother."

Serena nodded. She hugged Rosa awkwardly, her eyes lingering on the swollen arm. "I'm sorry I didn't come help," she said. "I wasn't really awake yet and I didn't realize what was going on." She hurried out of the room.

Grandmama began to rub the leaves over Rosa's arm. They were cool and took the itch away. Rosa stared at the tabletop and hoped that no one else was going to apologize to her today. She was getting very tired of holding everyone's apologies in her head.

When she'd rubbed every sting with the leaves, Grandmama dabbed honey on each of the spots. "Honey's got healing properties," she said. "It's practically magic. Nadia, you'd better put it on your ankle, too."

"I feel terribly weak," murmured Aunt Nadia. "As if the life was draining away from me...oh wait, it's just that there's no coffee."

Sergio made a rude noise and poured the freshly brewed coffee into her cup. The kitchen filled with the rich smell. Rosa sighed. She didn't like the taste, but the smell was heavenly.

"Now," said Grandmama. "Wiggle your fingers."

Rosa wiggled them. The skin no longer felt strange and tight. Her arm still had a vague itchy ache to it, and her elbow was stiff, but it seemed to be working. "I'm better!" she said.

"Don't overdo it," said Grandmama. "You should probably be in bed with hot tea, but the way things are going around here, I doubt there will be time for that."

Uncle Alfonso poked his head in the kitchen. "Marco is guarding the paintings," he said. "Serena told me what happened. I'm sorry I was so slow." He shook his head ruefully. "If it wasn't for you young people with your reflexes, we'd have lost the charcoal."

Rosa, Nadia and Sergio exchanged glances. Rosa felt a flush of pride to be one of the "young people."

Grandmama exhaled through her nose, the way she did when she was deciding not to be mad about something. Carefully not looking at Payne, she said "I think we've learned that we can't rely on just reflexes. Or any one person to stand guard. If it's so important that we keep this thing safe, we'll need to do more."

"It's true," said Rosa. "If it hadn't been for the chain, I think they'd have gotten it open."

"We could take it far away from here," said Uncle Alfonso, a bit doubtfully.

"The Scarling will come for it," said Payne. "It's drawn to it like a magnet."

"Better to fight on ground you know," said Uncle Marco. "They taught us that in the military. We live here. We know it better than the Scarling ever could."

"To say nothing of what that thing might do out in the world!" said Nadia. She shook her head. "It nearly gave me heart failure. Can you imagine what it might do to the old lady next door?"

"The *old lady next door* is younger than I am," said Grandmama acidly.

"This is excellent coffee," said Nadia hurriedly. "Truly excellent. Have I told you lately how much I admire your coffee?"

"Hmph!"

Payne shook his head miserably, unmoved by their banter. "I can't be relied upon to guard the box. If it wasn't for Rosa's radishes, we'd have lost everything. I've made a mess of this from beginning to end. I didn't want to tell anyone, and then I couldn't even be trusted to keep the box safe. You got *hurt* because of me. Tybalt should have painted a—a—*cat* on the box instead!"

Rosa reached out with her good hand and stroked the feathers on the back of his neck. "Payne—"

"It's true," said Grandmama, her voice like iron. "You're not wrong, crow. So what do you intend to do about it?"

Under Rosa's fingers, Payne shivered. "I can't make up for it," he said, turning his beak away.

"Nobody's asking you to," said Grandmama. Rosa hated that tone of voice. She'd used it on Rosa once or twice.

Rosa wanted to jump up, say something, change the

conversation so that she wouldn't have to hear Payne being yelled at. Her face burned in sympathetic embarrassment.

"If you were watching the box tonight," said Grandmama, "and the Scarling dangled gold and jewels and spoons in front of you, what would you do?"

"Nothing!" said Payne fiercely. "I wouldn't move a muscle! Not a feather! I wouldn't leave the box for anything!"

Grandmama reached out, flipped his beak up, and looked into his eyes.

Whatever she was looking for, apparently she found it. She grunted. "Good," she said. "Remember that. Now let's say no more about it."

The tension went out of the room like air let out of a balloon. Nadia set her coffee cup down with a *clunk*.

"So!" she said, brightly. "The chain was a good idea, but now they'll be expecting it. What are we going to do next?"

THIRTY-TWO

Morning
Watering Day
Thermidor, the Month of Heat

SERENA CAME BACK, out of breath, with a pair of cloths. The illuminations on them were golden-eyed lizards, holding red fruit in their front claws. One had a strawberry and one had an apple. Rosa knew from the *Codex* that it didn't matter what the fruit was, but it had to be red, and the lizards had to have golden eyes.

Illuminated bandages never lasted very long—you couldn't magically heal a broken arm with one, for example—but they helped. When Cousin Sergio had broken his left wrist last year, he'd drawn a new lizard on his cast every day. Eventually it had been completely covered in little green lizards holding red berries, everywhere he could reach. He'd had the cast off in two weeks and it had healed so cleanly that he barely had a scar.

"Mom says to yell if you need any more," said Serena.

Grandmama sighed. "I hope I won't," she said, "but I'm grateful for these. If they ever need a stuffed armadillo..."

Rosa looked away, as Grandmama wrapped her stiff arm in the healing cloth. The Studio Magnifico were their rivals. Everybody knew they were rivals. But apparently there was a difference between hoping to get a commission and refusing to give bandages to someone who'd been hurt. The studios might be rivals, but they went back and forth trading paint and canvas and—and—stuffed armadillos!

Because they were all illuminators together. Because everybody knew that when you needed paint, you needed it right now. And someday you'd be the one who needed to borrow paint...

"You must be feeling better," said Grandmama dryly. "You've been drumming your fingers on the table for five minutes."

"Oh!" Rosa looked down at her hand. Her fingers felt fine. When she stretched her arm out, her elbow made a sort of painful stretchy *twang*, but it moved.

Aunt Nadia stood up, paced across the room on her ankle, and sat down again. "Good as new," she said. "Though I probably won't go out dancing on it." She glanced at Payne. "Wings! In my next life, I shall have wings."

"Sensible," he said. "They're much more efficient."

"Leave the cloths on for a few more minutes, then we'll set them aside," ordered Grandmama. "Saint Fenester knows, we probably aren't getting through this without somebody else getting bit by a scribbling."

Serena looked smug. "My aunt did those," she said. "She's really good at it."

"I thought I recognized her style," said Grandmama. "Always does such lovely scales."

Payne cleared his throat. "About the box..."

"Have you figured out how to protect it yet?" asked Serena. Payne shook his head.

"Can't think!" said Sergio, standing up. "Going to guard the paintings! Send Marco in!"

He left the kitchen.

"Could we stick it down to something?" asked Rosa. "Like glue the box to the table?"

"Hmmm." Uncle Alfonso tapped the box thoughtfully. "That might be a good start. They'd have to get the box open instead of dragging it off to work on."

"Which shouldn't be too hard, honestly," said Payne. "It's just a latch, without the illumination on it...and I don't think Rosa can paint me back onto the box, unfortunately."

Rosa blinked. "You'd *want* to go back on the box?"

"I was a better guardian on it than I am off, apparently," said the crow dryly. "But it doesn't matter. I couldn't explain how Tybalt did it, so I imagine you're stuck with me to the end."

Rosa reached out and scratched his feathers. "I'm glad," she said. "I like having you around."

Payne rested his beak briefly along her hand.

"How *did* he do it?" asked Uncle Alfonso. "Not the magic, but the painting?"

"I sat in diluted turpentine until my paint started to dissolve," said Payne. "And I didn't enjoy that at all. It made my tailfeathers extremely sticky. Then I hopped onto the box and he started to push my paint around and things got very hazy. The next thing I knew, Rosa had figured out how to get the box open and I woke up again." He flicked his tail, as if to reassure himself that it was no longer sticky.

"How long do you think we have before it tries again?" asked Aunt Nadia.

"You kicked the Scarling pretty good," said Payne, with a little dip of his wings. "But his scribblings will only get weaker. I can't imagine he'll wait too long."

"There's no way he can make more scribblings?" asked Uncle Alfonso. "You're sure?"

"There's only the one piece of charcoal," said Payne doubtfully. "He shouldn't be able to. But there's a lot I don't know."

Rosa didn't think she'd ever heard Payne admit that before. She blinked at him. *Normally he's a worse know-it-all than Serena!*

"Suppose we just drop the whole box in wet cement?" said Aunt Nadia. "I'd like to see any drawing get it out of that!"

"That's a great idea!" said Serena, but Payne shook his head.

"We have to be able to get into the box ourselves," the crow said. "Otherwise it would be perfect. But Rosa has to be able to draw us more radishes." He nodded to the two leafy illuminations on the table. "They're the only thing we know will hold off the Scarling and its creatures."

"You think we'll need to hold more off?" asked Uncle Alfonso.

"I suspect we might," said Payne. "And it won't do us any good if it can't get into the box, if it's buried us under a pile of scribblings to get there."

Rosa thought of her family covered in scribblings, lying on the floor by a block of cement. It was a horrible image.

She tried to think of something else. What would be like cement, but easier to get into?

"What about clay?" she asked.

They all looked at her, puzzled.

"Clay?" said Aunt Nadia.

"What *about* clay?" asked Uncle Marco, limping into the kitchen.

"What if we wrapped the box in wet clay?" asked Rosa. "Really *thick* clay. Then we can pull it apart ourselves if we need to get into the box, but the scribblings will have to dig into it." The scribblings were pointy, but she didn't think lines would be very good for digging.

"Do we have any clay?" asked Grandmama.

"Sergio was building maquettes out of it last month," said Uncle Alfonso. (Maquettes were miniature sculptures, usually of humans, that a sculptor uses to work out ideas, like a rough sketch in clay. Cousin Sergio was not a very good sculptor, but he liked to do it sometimes as a change from painting. "Think differently!" he'd bark, hands in the clay. "Shake out cobwebs!")

"That's not a bad idea at all," said Uncle Marco. "I imagine it would slow them down quite a bit."

He put his hand on the back of the chair. "First, we'll need Rosa to draw us an army of radishes."

Cousin Sergio cleared his throat from the doorway. "Should see this!"

They all got up. Rosa carried the box in front of her and Payne rode on her shoulder.

Cousin Sergio led them into the main studio and pointed upward.

There was a collective indrawn breath. Rosa shivered.

"How long do you think it's been there?" asked Grandmama.

"Who knows?" asked Aunt Nadia grimly. "How often do any of us ever look up?"

"It wasn't there yesterday evening," said Payne. "I flew around before it got too dark."

In foot-high letters across the pale bricks, the Scarling had written:

WILL END STUPID MANDOLINIS FOR ALWAYS

"It's not very good grammar," said Serena.

Aunt Nadia glared into her coffee cup. "That'll be a consolation when we're all killed in our beds, I'm sure."

"No one's getting killed in their beds," said Uncle Marco.

He looked around at the rest of the family, at Serena, and nodded once. "From now on," he said, "nobody goes anywhere alone. We're at war."

THIRTY-THREE

Afternoon
Watering Day
Thermidor, the Month of Heat

THEY DRAGGED a table into the very center of the main studio. Rosa sat at the table with the box next to her and a pad of paper.

Her eyes kept being drawn up the wall to the Scarling's message. It was written in black charcoal.

Had the Scarling written the threat before it had come down and nearly been trapped? Or had it written it afterwards? And if it had been afterwards, what had it used?

It looked very much like the charcoal in her hand.

There can't be two pieces of charcoal, she thought. *If there's two, it'd be making more scribblings. If it's making more scrib-blings, then...*

She bent her head over the pad of paper and hastily drew a very large radish. She wasn't sure if bigger was better, but probably it couldn't hurt.

Grandmama and Cousin Sergio went into the kitchen and came back out with cups of tea for everyone. Uncle Marco and Alfonso pulled chairs up around the table. Everyone was careful not to stare at Rosa, which she appreciated, but she could feel the words on the wall watching her, like evil eyes.

"I didn't know the Scarling could write words," she said to Payne, as her radish drawing pulled itself away from the page.

"It can," said Payne. "It can't talk, so it writes."

"It's smarter than I thought, then."

"Well...." He tilted his wing back and forth in a maybe-yes, maybe-no gesture. "Not really. It's cunning, I suppose you'd say, not smart like a crow, or a person."

Rosa shaded in the leaves on another radish. She wasn't sure that she believed Payne. She had been thinking of the Scarling as something like a big, evil rat. Being able to read and write made you smarter than a rat, though, didn't it?

"What did it write when Tybalt had it?"

Payne shrugged. "Oh, you know. *Need more paper.* And *paint not dry.* That sort of thing."

"And it hates all Mandolinis because of this Tybalt person of yours? How lucky for us!"

Rosa stifled a sigh. When Aunt Nadia got sarcastic, there wasn't much that you could do.

Payne peered at her thoughtfully, turning his head. "You know..."

Nadia raised an eyebrow.

"You'd make a good crow," he told her, with the air of one bestowing a great compliment.

Nadia blinked at him, then broke into an unwilling smile.

A second radish climbed off the page. Rosa shook the cramps out of her hand and drank her tea. Grandmama had put honey in it.

Uncle Marco and Sergio had excavated the clay from the clutter under Sergio's desk. It was half dried out, and they had to dump water (and Sergio's tea) into the clay to get it wet again.

The two of them knelt down and began digging their hands into the clay to try to mix it. Sergio groaned. "Too dry! Need more!"

"It'll be fine," said Uncle Marco. "Keep kneading."

"It's called wedging if it's clay," said Serena, in that know-it-all tone that she had.

Uncle Marco was untroubled. "Keep wedging, then," he said. Sergio muttered something under his breath.

It was strange waiting for the Scarling to attack. Rosa had been keyed-up and scared and ready to fight, but it hadn't shown up. It had been over an hour. She didn't know how to feel. She had been ready to be heroic and now she just had to go to the bathroom, which didn't feel very heroic at all.

"It's funny," said Serena after a little while.

"What's funny?" asked Rosa. A little line of radishes had formed in front of her. They were grooming each other like cats, using their little fangs as if they were combs. It was cute and a little disturbing.

"There's a monster that's going to attack us and a talking painted crow and nasty little drawing-beasts...and the thing that'll save us is you drawing radishes. Just like we used to do on my bedroom floor."

She took a sheet of paper herself and dug out a pencil and began doodling a gryphon.

Rosa tried to smile. It wasn't easy. Her arm still hurt from the scribbling's attack. She was all too aware of the weight of everyone depending on her. It felt like wearing an itchy sweater that was too tight to move in. "I wish we were back in your bedroom drawing and none of us had ever heard of the Scarling."

Serena sighed. "Yeah. Me, too." She bent her head over the gryphon.

The sweater seemed to get even tighter, squeezing the words out of Rosa's chest. "You could go," she said. "Back home. I mean...you don't have to stay here. You've helped a lot already."

Serena blinked at her, and then drew herself up very straight. "A *Magnifico* does not *retreat*," she said. "Particularly not if a friend is in danger!"

"Bravo!" cried Cousin Sergio, still wrist deep in clay.

"Your grandfather would have been proud," said Uncle Marco. He grinned at Serena. "He died before you were born, I know, but we were great friends. It is good to see that our studios are still keeping that up."

Serena blushed and looked down at the gryphon.

Rosa set down the charcoal and reached out and squeezed her friend's arm. "We'll be friends even when we're grown-ups," she said.

Serena laughed. "And we'll talk about the time we fought scribble monsters and our grandkids won't believe us."

"That's the spirit," said Uncle Marco.

Another two radishes, and Rosa had to stop. Her fingers hurt from squeezing the charcoal too tightly. The last radish had come out a little crooked, with a root-nose that hung down like an elephant's trunk. The other radishes looked at it sympathetically and laid their leafy tails over its tail, making tiny papery chirps.

"Do you think that's enough?" she asked Payne. "I need a break..."

Payne spread his wings helplessly. "I don't know. I don't know how many scribblings it's got. I assume there can't be many left, and they've got to be getting hungry."

"I wish it would hurry up!" she said. "But I don't, either. I just—I want it over with!"

Uncle Marco rolled over on his stool and gripped her shoulder. "That's normal, Rosa. When I was in the army, we always said this was the worst part. Waiting for something to happen."

Payne nodded. "Honestly, I thought the Scarling would have attacked by now. Its army can't get any bigger, and they'll only get weaker over time."

"So what is it waiting for?" asked Rosa.

The painted crow sighed. "I don't know," he admitted. "And that worries me most of all."

THIRTY-FOUR

Evening
Watering Day
Thermidor, the Month of Heat

HOURS DRAGGED BY. Grandmama brought Rosa a bowl of hot water to soak her hands in. She was starting to feel light-headed.

"I don't think I can draw any more," she said finally. "I feel weird."

"Illumination fatigue," said Uncle Alfonso. "You should stop, then, Rosalita. You're young and strong, but you can't make an army."

"They say that the Reverend Mother of the Convent of the White Goat did," said Aunt Nadia, almost dreamily. "Barbarian raiders landed on her island, with only a handful of elderly nuns and novices to stand against them. She painted great canvases and mixed her own blood with the paint, to drape over the nuns like armor. Her illuminations made them impossible to kill and as strong as lions, and they drove off the barbarians, just the old women and the girls together." She looked down into her coffee cup and gave a small, unhappy laugh. "And the Reverend Mother died that night of exhaustion, from pouring so much of herself into the illuminations. They buried her under the altarstone, and her paintbrushes are treated like the relics of a saint."

"It's an old story," said Uncle Alfonso. "I don't know that there's any truth to it."

"We're trying to avoid having people die," said Grandmama testily. "Particularly Rosa. Really, Nadia!"

Aunt Nadia grinned, unrepentant. "I think our Rosa would make a fine warrior nun, actually."

"Won't work!" said Cousin Sergio.

"Eh?"

"Blood and paint! Wouldn't mix well!" He shook his head. "Would get all clumpy! Bad idea!"

"Ewwww!" said Serena, wrinkling her nose.

"I imagine you could do it with watercolor, though," said Aunt Nadia. "Or egg tempera."

"Tempera might work!" Sergio allowed.

"*No one is bleeding on the paint,*" Grandmama snapped. "Really, you two! Rosa, stop drawing and I'll bring you some food."

Rosa set the charcoal inside the box and closed the latch. Uncle Marco scooted his stool over and began smoothing clay over the join.

"Well," said Aunt Nadia, "if the monsters aren't going to oblige us by showing up at a decent hour, I need a nap."

The last word was barely out of her mouth when Uncle Alfonso shouted "Look out!" and flung himself over Rosa.

A shower of objects fell from the ceiling. Serena took cover under the table.

The Scarling was attacking at last.

ROSA HEARD Uncle Alfonso grunt as something struck him. Aunt Nadia joined Serena under the table. Uncle Marco threw his body over the box on the table and Sergio tried to shield Grandmama.

Rosa was wedged under her uncle's armpit. She could see the things falling just past her nose. It looked like silverware, mixed with pencils, cups, a stuffed hummingbird, and other small objects that the scribblings had scavenged from around the studio.

That's why they took so long to attack. They were gathering up things to throw at us!

The elephant-nosed radish galloped over and took up a guard position in front of Rosa's face. It was faintly transparent, so she could still see through it. The other radishes were gathered under the table, except for two who were trying to shield Uncle Marco.

She heard Payne cawing angrily from somewhere behind her.

After a minor eternity, the rain of household artillery tapered off. There was silence in the studio. Uncle Alfonso sat up and let Rosa out from under him. A nick on his forehead was starting to bleed and he dabbed at it with his sleeve.

"Payne," said Grandmama, from somewhere under Cousin Sergio, "I'm not sure what you were saying, but I suspect I should wash your beak out with soap."

"Rawwk!" said Payne. "I can't fly when the air is full of things! It's like trying to get aloft in a hailstorm."

"Everyone all right?" asked Uncle Alfonso. "No one hurt?"

"Get off me, Sergio, you're squashing me."

"Some cuts and bruises. Nothing major. The radishes kept me from taking a mug to the head," said Uncle Marco.

"Nadia and I are fine," said Serena. "I think."

"I am *not* fine," said Aunt Nadia. "I didn't get a nap and my coffee has spilt. Also, if you look up, there seem to be a great many of them."

Everyone looked up.

The bricks were lined with scribblings. There were dozens, maybe even hundreds. Most of them looked—normal? But there were four or five enormous ones that were nearly as tall as Rosa.

Their outlines were crisp and black. They stared down facelessly at the humans below. One had spikes all over and one had no head, but a giant mouth in the middle of its chest. One had four arms with huge, three fingered hands.

"Payne," said Rosa. Her voice sounded very thin in her own ears. "Payne, those are *fresh*."

"I see them," said Payne. He hopped over to her and flapped up to her shoulder. "But you've still got the charcoal."

Rosa nodded.

"So that means that there must be another charcoal, right?" said Uncle Marco.

The scribblings stared down at them. A faint chittering drifted down, like quiet, malicious laughter.

Payne shook his head slowly, not in negation, but in disbelief. "There must be," he said. "But there can't be. I don't understand. The first one was made from the Scarling's own roots. How can there be more than one?"

Serena pointed.

The Scarling stood atop one of the bay walls. It was holding up something that looked like a small burnt stick. The end was curled and twisted like a root.

"Mother of god," breathed Uncle Marco.

The Scarling's other arm was missing.

"IT CUT off its own root and burned it?" said Uncle Marco.

Payne's eyes were huge. "I *guess* that might work—but it can't be very good—it may not last like the first one?"

"It doesn't have to last forever," said Aunt Nadia dryly. "Just long enough to bury us in angry drawings."

Payne closed his beak with a snap.

"Bad!" said Cousin Sergio. "Very bad!"

"If it's got what it wants, why doesn't it leave?" asked Serena. "It can feed itself and make more scribblings now, can't it?"

Rosa's eyes were drawn back to the huge scribblings. Through the one with the spikes, she could still make out the words WILL END STUPID MANDOLINIS FOR ALWAYS.

"That's not what it really wants," she said quietly. "It wants revenge."

"Revenge for what?" asked Uncle Marco. "All Tybalt did was pay more attention to someone else."

Rosa shook her head. "No. That's what started it. But it's been locked in a box for two hundred years."

She wondered if a grown-up would understand. Grown-ups never seemed to get bored. Maybe they'd forgotten how boredom could twist around and become a horrible gray blanket that lay over everything until you were climbing the walls trying to find ways to keep yourself entertained.

"Look," she said, "you always say 'You'll understand when you're older.' But you'd understand if you were younger! How bored and angry can it get in two hundred years? The Scarling couldn't go play outside! All it could do was sit there and get madder and madder and think of ways to get revenge!"

Serena looked at her. Her face had gone white, and Rosa wondered if her friend was regretting saying that Magnificos did not retreat.

She reached out and took Serena's hand and squeezed. Serena was shaking. Rosa looked down at their joined hands and realized that she was, too.

"I can't believe it tore off its own arm..." mumbled Serena. "That's *horrible*."

"It's an evil mandrake root with a painted clown face that's sworn to kill us all," said Aunt Nadia. "And *the arm's* the bit that's bothering you?"

Rosa laughed. She didn't mean to, it just came out. Serena stared at her, and flushed, and then she laughed too.

It helped. It wasn't funny, exactly, but it made her feel better.

On some level, Rosa knew that she was frightened. She could feel the fear in her stomach. But it seemed to all be staying down there, and her mind felt very clear.

That's okay. As long as I can still think, that's okay.

The Scarling brandished its burnt charcoal arm overhead. The clown mouth curved upward in a hideous grin.

The chittering grew louder. It came in waves, over and over, and Rosa realized that the scribblings were cheering.

Over and over they cheered, as the Scarling stabbed its burnt arm into the air. Then it stopped, and silence fell across the studio.

Nobody was laughing any more.

Slowly, slowly, the Scarling lowered the arm until it pointed. At Rosa. At Payne. At her family.

The Scarling's painted mouth cracked open and it hissed.

The chittering grew to a roar, and the scribblings flung themselves down from the walls and threw themselves across the open floor, toward the painters of the Studio Mandolini.

THIRTY-FIVE

Rosa's first instinct was to hide under the table. She had just started to duck down when it occurred to her that there was no reason to protect the charcoal now, if the Scarling had another one. She snatched the box off the table and then dove underneath.

The clay was most of the way around the lid. Uncle Marco had stopped before he quite finished. Rosa clawed at the seal, trying to get it open.

The clay was horribly effective. Rosa's idea had been a very good one. Unfortunately.

Stupid good idea! she thought furiously. Dark brown half-moons appeared under her fingernails as she tore at it.

All around the table, the sounds of battle were rising. Cousin Sergio had his big palette knives in both hands and was stabbing and slashing at the scribblings. Aunt Nadia was stomping them and kicking them with her heavy boots. Uncle Marco was on his wheeled stool, rolling over the smaller ones and flailing at the big ones with the half-full bag of clay. It was like a weighted club made out of linen. He whacked one of the big ones in the midsection with it and the scribbling flew backwards, charcoal dust puffing from its lines. It screeched in pain.

"I meant to grab a hammer!" Uncle Marco shouted, half to himself. "Why didn't I grab one earlier?"

"You never did plan ahead very well!" snapped Grandmama. She had armed herself from the kitchen and had a ladle in one hand and a wickedly pronged fork in the other. "Fortunately, you're good at improvising!"

It was true. Uncle Marco bashed the clay down into a pile of scribblings and left charcoal streaks on the floor. They apparently could not stand up to being bashed hard with ten pounds of clay.

Payne swooped overhead, diving at the giant scribblings and forcing them to stop and cover their heads (at least, the ones that had heads).

Rosa's radishes formed ranks around the table, trying to keep the scribblings from getting to her. One scribbling that was mostly claws and eyes leapt over them and reached for her, but was immediately buried under a wave of fangs and leaves.

With a sob of relief, Rosa tore the last strip of clay away and threw the box open. She scrabbled for the charcoal, found it, and flung the box away.

Two more of the giant scribblings had come down from the wall. They were standing shoulder to shoulder and shoving Cousin Sergio back, trying to cut him off from the rest of the Mandolinis.

We need big defenders! I don't have any paper—I need—I need—

No, wait, I'm sitting on the biggest canvas of all!

Rosa scooted backward, drawing the outline of a radish around herself on the floor. The radish was nearly as big as the table. She didn't dare go much bigger, or she'd have to come out from under the table.

Aunt Nadia came to Sergio's rescue. "That's my nephew, you wretch!" she cried, and brought her coffee mug down on a giant scribbling's head. It staggered and Sergio slashed at it with the palette knives, tearing pale lines across the flickering shape. The scribbling roared with a ripping sound, like someone slicing open a canvas.

Another scribbling jumped the line of radishes. It landed on Rosa's shoulder and she had a brief view of a crudely drawn mouth opening to bite, and then Serena clobbered it with her shoe.

Her friend crouched down beside her. There was a radish on top of her head. "Keep drawing!" she said. "I'll keep them off you!"

"Thank you!" said Rosa. Her fingers felt like electric sparks were shooting up her wrist, but that didn't matter. She scrawled leaves with jagged edges on the floor. Serena smacked another scribbling aside with her shoe. The radishes made space for her in their line.

Rosa could only watch the battle from the corner of her eye. The radishes formed a circle around the table, guarding Rosa, and the scribblings were making a determined effort to get through to the charcoal.

She scrawled fangs practically under her knees and then leaned over to draw a hasty halo. A scribbling leapt for her elbow and two radishes brought it crashing down.

She joined the halo line to the radish's back, then laid both hands flat against the floor. She still wasn't sure how you made an illumination—it seemed like a thing that just happened and made you tired—but she needed this one to *work*.

Aunt Nadia yelped, falling back against the table. There were scribblings clinging to her legs. Radishes swarmed up her calves, pulling them off, but it made a gap in the line.

Serena moved to fill the space, shoe swinging.

Please, Rosa thought at her drawing. *Please be big and strong and powerful. My family needs help.*

The radishes pulled the scribblings off Nadia, but her skirt was torn and covered in charcoal. One of the radishes was down, lying flat and half-erased on the ground. Another was missing most of its leaves. The sight filled Rosa with anguish. She was drawing them to fight for the studio, of course, but she wanted them all to live! It was terrible to draw something and bring it to life just so the Scarling could kill it!

But if I don't, the Scarling will kill us all if it can. And it'll get into the city and eat illuminations until everything goes terribly, terribly wrong.

She closed her eyes and willed the giant drawing to get up.

Rosa actually *felt* the illumination take. She was suddenly exhausted, right down to the bone. She felt herself swaying and opened her eyes, just in time to see the radish pull itself off the ground.

The giant drawing passed through her, still only half-solid. It felt like walking into fog, like a faceful of cobwebs, but somehow *friendly* instead of nasty. It felt like a sunbeam made solid.

It shook itself and grew more and more solid, fanning out its leaves, and then it was too large to be under the table and had to wriggle out, with the table sliding over its back and thumping back down as it got free.

There was a sudden pause in combat. Scribblings turned to look at the new arrival. So did the Mandolinis.

"Oh my," said Grandmama.

"Rosalita, you've outdone yourself," said Uncle Alfonso.

The giant radish gave a baritone chirp. Tiny radishes swirled around it, rubbing against it like kittens with a big dog.

"Nice!" cried Cousin Sergio, and stabbed his palette knife in the air.

The very large scribblings all took a very large step backward and looked worriedly at the Scarling.

With a scream of wordless rage, the mandrake root swung down from the wall and began dragging its burnt arm across the plaster, scrawling eyes, teeth, claws, anything horrible and jagged and unpleasant.

Rosa slumped backward. She knew that she should try to draw another radish, but she couldn't. Her arm was stabbing with pain and she was so *tired*.

Aunt Nadia dropped down beside her. "Rosa?"

Rosa shook her head. The room was spinning. She groped for Nadia's hand and pressed the charcoal into it. "Don't...don't let..."

"The big one was too much," said Serena over her shoulder. "I think she's going to faint."

Rosa wanted to say, indignantly, that she had never fainted in her life, but it seemed like that would take a lot of energy.

"Get her over here," said Uncle Alfonso. He grabbed the edge of the table and began to drag it backwards, toward the nearest bay. Rosa crawled along with it, with Serena helping her.

She could understand why he was moving it—with the suddenly increased army of scribblings, they were badly outnumbered. It would be much easier to defend a bay than a table in the middle of the room.

It still made her feel exposed, as if he was taking her shield away and she was having to scurry after it. And she was so very, very tired.

At last—it seemed like a year later—he stopped. The bay was close behind them. The small scribblings might still come over the walls, but the big ones would have a harder time getting to them.

Aunt Nadia had crawled along with them. Her leg was dragging behind her, the knee already swelling. She wasn't paying any attention to it. Instead she stared at the charcoal in her hands, turning it over and over.

Serena reached up on top of the table, grabbed a mug of tea that somehow had not been overturned, and pressed it to Rosa's lips.

"Payne," said Nadia slowly. "Payne! Crow!"

"What?" cried Payne. He broke away from battling the scribblings on top of the table. Rosa could hear his claws clacking as he hopped. "What is it?"

"You said Tybalt's gift was rare."

"It is!"

"You said that it was so rare that only Rosa could do it—and we believed you."

"What?" said Payne.

"You were wrong about the Scarling's charcoal," said Aunt Nadia. "Rosa's my brother's daughter. The same blood's in all our veins. And look!"

She pointed.

She had crawled across the floor with the charcoal in her hand, and it had left a jagged, awkward line on the tiles.

The scribblings were lashing furiously at the lines.

"It's not an illumination, though," said Payne. "It's just lines. It's just—why *are* they doing that?" He sounded baffled.

"I could feel it," said Aunt Nadia. "It was when I went over the illumination against rats." She started to laugh. "It's old and it needs replacing and as soon as the charcoal hit it, it was like I had started working on repairing it. I could *feel* the magic."

"It's not possible," said Payne, but he sounded uncertain now.

Her swollen knee was stuck out to one side, so Aunt Nadia had to kneel awkwardly on one leg. She began to draw—not a radish, but an angel.

"I thought the radishes were the illumination against scribblings," said Serena.

"I'm bad at radishes," said Nadia. "I'm quite good at angels. And we need a proof of concept."

Her angel had powerful wings with a suggestion of feathers. The face was hastily drawn and slightly lopsided, but smiling. Nadia set her hand on the drawing, much like Rosa had, and murmured something under her breath that Rosa couldn't quite hear.

The Scarling's scream was louder this time, like an enraged monkey. Its monstrous scribbling began to peel off the wall, just as Nadia's angel came to life.

It flew out from under the table and took its place alongside Cousin Sergio. It was only about two feet tall, but it hovered in the air beside him. Nadia had thoughtfully given the angel a sword, which it brandished at the cowed scribblings.

Payne drew in his breath. "You can do it too..." he said, sounding awestruck.

Nadia let out a short, huffy laugh. "And shame on me for

not trying before, instead of working Rosa to the bone!" She started on a second angel.

The scribblings shook themselves out of their surprise and waded forward. The giant radish, the angel, and Cousin Sergio met them. The studio filled with chirps and chitters and a high, brittle singing that could only be the angel.

Paper flew. Uncle Marco plowed into a giant scribbling on his stool, knocking it to the ground, and the radish rolled over it like a barrel. The angel laid about itself with the charcoal sword and Cousin Sergio's palette knives rose and fell. The scribbling with the face in the middle of its chest went down, half-erased.

For a moment it seemed as if the tide of battle was turning their way...but then the huge scribbling waded into the fray.

It had hands like hammers. One blow knocked Nadia's angel flying. Cousin Sergio threw himself flat and had to scramble backwards to keep from being trampled.

The radishes formed a defensive line as the Mandolinis fell back to the table. Grandmama was limping but still brandished her ladle fiercely.

Nadia's second angel came to life. She slumped backward against the leg of the table and looked over at Rosa. "That's exhausting. Much worse than just a regular illumination. How did you make so *many?*"

"Our Rosalita's young and strong," said Uncle Alfonso. He leaned against the table, watching the radishes battle the scribblings. "Pass the charcoal up here, will you, Nadia?"

She did. He drew directly on the table. Rosa, beginning to feel a bit better, poked her head over the edge and saw that he was drawing something that looked vaguely like a badger, with a radish riding on its back.

"Will that work?" she asked.

"Haven't a clue," he admitted. "But it's doing something... oh, look there!"

His badger and riding radish sparkled. Alfonso put his hand onto it and Rosa thought that he was pushing power at it, the same way she had with her giant radish earlier.

It rose off the table and let out a papery roar. The badger had huge claws, which it waved in the air. The radish rattled its leaves fiercely.

The drawing was only about two feet high—the table wasn't that large—but it leapt down and charged into battle. The scribblings recoiled from it the way that they did from the radishes. It slashed at the hammer-handed giant's ankles with its claws.

Uncle Alfonso, too, slumped, this time against the wall of the bay behind the table. "My goodness," he said. "That was... like a whole mural's worth of energy being pulled out at once."

"*Three* of you?" said Payne in disbelief.

"We're *all* Tybalt's descendants," said Aunt Nadia. "Sergio! Try one! Do the radish, though, those work much better than angels."

Sergio snatched the charcoal away and set to work. After a minute, Grandmama whacked him on the shoulder with her ladle. "You don't need to shade every scale!" she said. "This is not the time for perfectionism!"

The giant lifted its hammer and roared, bringing it down on the giant radish. The radish vanished in a shower of charcoal dust.

Rosa felt a strange pang in her chest and cried out, just as the giant radish fell beneath the hammer-handed giant. She actually *felt* it, as if somebody had flicked her heart with their finger.

"It's no good," she said, watching the giant stomp forward. "We need something bigger."

"I don't know if any of us can make something bigger," said Nadia. "It takes so much energy..." She shook her head. There were dark circles under her eyes that hadn't been there a few minutes ago.

The tabletop shifted. Something very weird slid off it. The front half looked like one of Rosa's radishes, but the back half was an enormous snake. Sergio was still trying to draw scales on it as it slithered away.

"Your cousin's *weird*," whispered Serena.

"Yeah, but he's a genius."

"He's a *weird* genius."

Cousin Sergio slid down the wall, clutching the charcoal. He gave Serena and Rosa a weak grin. "*Tired* genius!"

As the radish-snake unrolled, the genius of it became more obvious. Sergio had doubled the tail back on itself over and over, using every inch of the tabletop. The radish-snake was nearly fifteen feet long.

It spread its fangs and hissed at the hammer-handed giant.

Uncle Marco was up next. His radish looked suspiciously like a beetle and the leaves strongly resembled insect wings, but it came to life and skittered, clicking, into battle.

He grunted. "That does have a kick to it. Anyone else?"

"Not me," said Grandmama. "I never had any gift for illuminating. Which is fine! Somebody has to keep all you brilliant artists fed!"

She cracked her ladle down onto a scribbling that was trying to sneak into the bay.

"Is it working?" asked Rosa. The studio was becoming a mass of battling charcoal lines. It was hard to tell who was winning. She could see that Nadia's angels were no longer in the air, but the space around the giant scribblings was a mass of tangled lines. The radish-snake was constricting the hammer-hand and looked to be winning.

"It could be better," said Aunt Nadia. She hopped on her good foot. "That nasty little root's drawing another big one. Why doesn't *it* get tired?"

"It's a creature of living magic—" Payne began.

"Payne," said Rosa severely, "are you sure? You're not just guessing again, like with the charcoal?"

The crow looked abashed. "I...um. Well. Err...I *think* the Scarling's yanking all the power out of the little ones to make the big ones."

The hammer-hand, still half-strangled by the radish-snake, brought its fists down on the badger. The badger and its radish rider vanished in an explosion of charcoal dust.

The Scarling was sketching furiously. The drawing on the wall was even larger than the hammer-hand, a hunched over monster with grasping claws and enormous teeth.

Only the radish-snake, Marco's beetle, and a handful of smaller radishes clustered around the table remained of the Mandolini's defenders.

"We'll have to do another one," said Uncle Marco grimly.

"It's not enough," said Aunt Nadia. "It's wearing us out faster than we're wearing it out. I don't know that any of us have the strength."

And then Serena said, "Why don't you do one together?"

THIRTY-SIX

THE MANDOLINIS STARED AT HER.

Serena tossed her hair back, looking annoyed. Her forehead was smudged with dust and she kept shaking her left hand, where a scribbling had gotten her on the wrist.

"We do it all the time at Studio Magnifico. You've got a big project, a bunch of you work on it. It's how we did those tiles for the water system project, you remember?"

"Out of the mouths of babes," muttered Uncle Marco.

"Yes," said Uncle Alfonso. "Yes. That is a good thought. All of us together."

He looked at the charcoal, and then handed it to Rosa. "And Rosalita should draw it."

"Me?" squeaked Rosa.

"Your radishes are what is saving us," said Uncle Alfonso. "You've got the best chance. Draw the biggest one you can, and the rest of us will give you all our power."

"You'll each need to add a little to it," said Serena.

"And Serena and I shall make sure you have the time to do so," said Grandmama. She linked elbows with Serena and hefted her ladle high.

Rosa gulped. "I'll need more space," she said.

They were in Aunt Nadia's bay. Nadia grabbed the giant painting of angels and flung it toward the back, heedless of the damage to the image, revealing a bare wall behind it.

"Nadia, your angels!"

"The one on the left wasn't working anyway!" snapped Aunt Nadia. "And if we're all dead, I certainly won't make my deadline! Now help me clear the walls!"

She attacked the opposite wall like a wrecking ball, yanking down the cards and bits of sketches pinned up on the plaster. Alfonso and Sergio leapt to help her.

Rosa turned the charcoal over in her fingers.

The biggest one I can...

She took a deep breath and began to draw.

Cousin Sergio was right behind her. He crouched down on the floor, waiting.

Rosa got the root-like face of the radish in, and the long fangs. She could feel the illumination pulling at her, like a deep current in the water, drawing her energy to bring itself to life.

She paused and passed the charcoal to Sergio. He thought for an instant, then drew a half dozen small, precise scales along the top of the radish's head.

He handed the charcoal back to her. As soon as she touched the tip to the line, she felt Sergio's energy flooding through her.

It was *fast*. Sergio's power was like a hummingbird, moving at twice the speed of the people around him, a swift, fiery blaze.

No wonder he talks so fast—and it's hard for us to under-

stand him sometimes! He jumps from one thing to the next so quickly because he sees all these connections and doesn't understand why the rest of us can't follow along.

Rosa drew the line along the floor to the wall, then up as far as she could reach in a great round curve. At the top, Uncle Alfonso took the charcoal and swept it along the wall, and then his magic, too, was added to the illumination they were building.

His was a far steadier power than Cousin Sergio's, as deep and slow as the bedrock that the city was built on. It anchored the illumination and gave it a solid place to stand. At the same time, images flicked through Rosa's mind, too quick to follow—scenes of a long life lived gladly and well, an incredible depth of knowledge, and a love for his family that warmed her like a cup of hot chocolate on a cold day. His power grounded her, slowing the sudden hummingbird-race of Rosa's heart, offering shelter from the terrible storm of magic around them.

Alfonso pulled the line down until she could reach it, and she took it to the floor and began to scribble in the leaves.

Outside of the bay, she heard the Scarling screaming in rage. Serena let out a yelp, and Grandmama said a very bad word indeed.

It all seemed to be very far away. *We must finish this,* thought Rosa dreamily. *I must save them.*

She finished the rough shape of the leaves and handed the charcoal to Uncle Marco.

He drew in the veins, half-leaves, half-beetle wings, and suddenly Rosa knew things about Uncle Marco that she had never suspected—how much his bad leg hurt him and how much he feared being a burden on his family, how he sought escape in paint, because in art, it did not matter if you had to walk with a cane or not.

The energy that surged into her from her uncle was so determined that it was terrifying. It was a warrior spirit, hammered and forged like steel.

"Why are you an artist?" demanded Rosa. "You should be leading armies!" Uncle Marco laughed.

"I may have done something of the sort in my youth," he said, as Rosa began to draw the shape of the radish on the opposite wall, and suddenly there was an image, right there in her head, and Rosa was looking down at a line of men with swords, sweeping their blades up in salute. "But that was long ago and far away."

Rosa began to fear that, far from not having enough power, the combined might of Studio Mandolini might overwhelm her. It was flowing through her, incredibly strong, the personalities of her family blending together into one great roar of love and strength and art. It threatened to sweep her away. She clung to the charcoal as if it were an anchor.

Just...got to finish...

She joined the lines together. Only the halo was left to finish.

Aunt Nadia took the charcoal—Nadia, who painted angels —and held Rosa upright with her free arm. "Together," she said, and began to draw the halo in.

Rosa did not know what she had expected from Aunt Nadia—something prickly and spiky, perhaps—but what she found was that the prickliness was a narrow-armored shell over a bright flame. Hers was a soul that would gladly burn itself out in pursuit of art, and then give the art away at the end, because it was the act of creating that mattered, the act that made her feel alive.

Rosa reached out and closed her fingers over her aunt's, and together they drew the last line of the halo to the body of the illumination.

THE FLOW of power instantly doubled. Rosa thought that she might have screamed, mostly in surprise. It didn't hurt, any more than being swept out to sea hurt, but it was shockingly powerful.

She knew that she had to funnel that power into the illumination, but she wasn't sure how. Before this morning, she'd never even made a full illumination before.

She opened her eyes—she hadn't realized that she'd closed them—and saw the charcoal line around the great radish glowing silver.

What did that remind her of...?

In her mind's eye, she saw the illuminated tiles fitting together at the water tunnel, the golden light rising from them, and the way the light had driven back the great wave of filth inside the water, like a monstrous serpent cowering away from the light.

The Mandolinis' power working together was the color of moonlight, but just as strong as the golden light had been.

We can do this, she thought. Hope surged inside her, and the light flared brighter than ever.

More, she thought at the great illumination. *More. Get up. Get up and fight for us. I order you—*

No. No, that was the wrong thing to say. You didn't order your art to do something, you *asked* it. Sometimes you begged.

And sometimes it didn't work, but when it did, if you were lucky, there was that transcendent moment when everything flowed and you couldn't put a brushstroke wrong, and all the Studio Mandolini was with Rosa and she reached out and whispered, *"Please."*

The magic roared around her. The radish began to wiggle against the floor and the magic was flowing now, like the tide, and Rosa could barely stand against it.

The Scarling's screams, which she'd been vaguely aware of, changed in pitch. Rosa looked up, and saw that the beast it had drawn was coming to life. A ruin of fallen scribblings lay at its feet, dissolving into charcoal.

It stood up...and up...and up...

Its head nearly brushed the rafters. Its wickedly clawed arms were folded up like a preying mantis.

Please get up! thought Rosa desperately to the radish.

Grandmama and Serena were all that stood between them and the mantis monster. They looked tiny and fragile and fierce.

It flexed its claws and took a step forward. Grandmama raised her ladle in defiance. Serena had—oh lord, Serena was going to try to fight the monster off with her shoe.

No! thought Rosa, and flung everything she had into the great illumination before her.

She stopped trying to fight against the magical current and dove into it instead. If she was lost, swept out to sea, vanished forever, that was fine. She would not allow the Scarling to hurt her family and her friend.

The great radish moved.

She felt it pull away from the wall, felt its shadowy body pass through the Mandolinis like friendly mist.

And then it was alive.

The mantis claws swept down toward the defenders—and a mass of leaves went over them like a shield.

The claws bounced off. The leaves were as tough as beetle shell, it seemed, a gift of Uncle Marco and his time spent drawing Walter.

The great radish shoved the table aside, nudged Grandmama and Serena out of danger, and smashed itself into the mantis monster.

Rosa swayed on her feet.

The mantis struck down, tearing a gouge in the great radish's body, and Rosa poured more magic into it, trying to heal the lines. Silver mist fizzed across the illumination's body. The charcoal lines strengthened, though a blurriness remained around them. It looked as if someone had smudged a line out with their finger and then redrawn it over the top of the original.

The radish slammed sideways into the mantis-monster, knocking it off its feet. Grandmama and Serena took advantage of its distraction to pick themselves up and run. They went hunched over, trying not to attract its attention, and dove into Cousin Sergio's bay, next to Nadia's.

"Are you all right?" called Uncle Alfonso.

"Fine!" called Grandmama. "Serena's young and I'm well-padded."

The mantis struggled to rise and the great radish rolled over the top of it. Its halo sparkled silver.

Rosa was in a place beyond words. She no longer thought at her illumination, she simply *felt* at it, sending strength and love and the desire for the battle to end. Her legs had given out, but that was okay. Someone was holding her up.

The mantis stabbed upward with its claws at the great radish. The radish twisted like a gigantic, leafy cat and struck back with its fangs.

It was eerily silent in the studio. No one spoke. Illumination struggled against illumination, scrabbling and striking and then...

...the mantis broke. Its lines faded as if they were being erased, and then it simply fell apart into a shower of charcoal dust.

The Scarling screamed in rage, stabbing its twisted piece of charcoal at the air—and Payne struck.

His talons closed around the charcoal, trying to wrench it away from the Scarling, but the mandrake root refused to let go. Crow and monster tumbled through the air together, Payne's wings flapping furiously as he tried to stay aloft. The Scarling struck at him, shrieking in its high, chittering voice.

They hit the floor, bounced, rolled, rose up, and fell again. Payne cawed furiously.

"Payne!" cried Grandmama.

The crow drove his beak down against the Scarling's arm. The root flailed.

It did not release the charcoal, but the arm holding it tore free.

The Scarling fell. Payne careened through the air gracelessly, holding the Scarling's charcoal, and flopped to the ground inside the bay.

Grandmama slammed her ladle down on the Scarling's wooden head.

"That's for attacking my granddaughter!" she shouted, smacking it again. "And that's for Payne—and that's for Nadia's painting—and that's for ruining all those illuminations so the whole place smelled like garbage—"

The Scarling reeled.

"It's down!" cried Aunt Nadia. "It's down—Serena! Get the box!"

Serena scrambled under the table, searching frantically for the crow box.

"Rosa, you can stop!"

Rosa was lost in the magic. Too much power had flowed through her. She could not remember anything except the need to direct it all into the illumination.

"Rosa, stop!"

Who is Rosa? she thought vaguely.

"Everyone!" said a voice. "Everyone, focus on Rosa! We're losing her!"

The magic changed.

The wave that had swept through her for so long had been about art, and the love of art, the joy of paint spread on canvas and lines drawn on paper.

Now it was the love of Rosa.

She saw herself reflected in four sets of eyes, Marco and Alfonso and Sergio and Nadia, a mirror far kinder than any piece of glass. She saw her uncle's delight in her curiosity and her cousin's fierce desire to protect her from harm and her aunt's sneaky glee in having another girl around the studio that she could lock eyes with and roll her eyes and go, "Men!"

A voice came to her, through the waves of power.

Rosalita, it said. *You are our Rosalita and we love you. Come back to us.*

I am...?

She was not quite sure who she was, but she found that she

very much wanted to be the Rosa that she saw in her family's minds. That person seemed like a very good person to be.

I am...Rosa?

Yes! cried her family, as one. *Yes, you are!*

I am Rosa!

She drew in a deep shuddering breath, nearly a sob, and she felt as if she were falling back into her body from a great height. "Yes!" she said aloud, and began to cough. Her lungs felt full of charcoal dust.

Its duty done, the great radish lifted its leaves in salute and faded away, until it was only a shadow in a sunbeam. Dust motes danced through it, an unexpected shade of silver.

"But...what happened to the Scarling...?" gasped Rosa.

Cousin Sergio blinked. Aunt Nadia looked around.

Serena cleared her throat.

She was holding the box, with the lid snapped shut. Payne crouched atop it with his feathers sticking up in all directions, looking rather the worse for wear. Grandmama was cleaning bits of bark off her ladle.

"We caught it," she said. "It's over. We won."

THIRTY-SEVEN

Morning
Puffball Day
Fructidor, the Month of Orchards

THE OPENING for the great fountain in front of the Dynast's palace was attended by cheering crowds, minor nobles, and enterprising vendors selling meat on a stick. Rosa and Serena stood arm in arm, well back from the fountain. They could just see, over the crowd, sparkling water being thrown high into the air.

The water came from the canals, newly cleaned by the magic of the illuminations. The Dynast himself came down and drank it from a silver cup, and people threw their hats into the air, and then spent several minutes sheepishly trying to locate their hats afterwards.

When the crowd had mostly dispersed, Serena's brother came and leaned against the building next to them. The square was emptying rapidly, except for a few forlorn hats.

"Well," he said. "That's a relief. I drank the water myself and I was certain it was safe, but you still hate to poison your city's ruler."

Rosa and Serena both giggled. He looked over at them and cocked an eyebrow. "Good to see that you two are friends again."

"Uh-huh," said Rosa.

"*Best* friends," said Serena.

It was true. They still quibbled occasionally—people are human, after all—but there were no more fights. Rosa had only to remember the scribblings trying to stab at her drawing hand and Serena bashing them aside with her shoe—and then standing beside Grandmama, gazing up at the mantis-monster, and whatever they might fight over didn't seem important any longer.

She didn't know what Serena thought of in those moments. One day perhaps she'd ask.

They did not play warriors or great beauties any longer. Mostly, they drew together in companionable silence.

Serena *had* started to say, "You'll understand when you're older," once, and then stopped herself. Rosa couldn't even remember what it had been now, just that Serena had stopped. Maybe for some things, it didn't matter how old you were.

"You know, it was odd," said her brother. He glanced at them both again, his eyes dark and shrewd. "We did another set of illuminations on the fountain, you know, right after they poured the foundation, to keep all the pipes in place and make sure nothing went bad."

Rosa and Serena both went very still.

"A *very* potent set of illuminations, I thought," he said. "More so than usual for a little construction project like this. Sergio insisted on it. And you know, when we set the last one in, and the magic took...it felt as if it were holding something *down*."

Serena and Rosa looked at each other, then back at the illuminator.

"Probably just your imagination," said Serena, without much conviction.

"Cousin Sergio gets these ideas, you know," said Rosa.

"But he's a genius," said Serena stoutly. "So it was probably a good idea."

"Mmm," said her brother. "He is. I suppose you two wouldn't know anything about it, would you?"

"Oh no."

"Certainly not."

He nodded. "That's what I thought."

The girls watched him wander away, whistling.

He went by the fountain, stepping on a newly laid stretch of paving stones. They were set in concrete. He might have been surprised by just how deep the concrete went—or then again, perhaps he wouldn't.

The Scarling's box was now buried in concrete in the foundation of a massive public works project. It seemed unlikely that anyone would dig it up for a thousand years or so.

"And that's as good as anyone can do," Grandmama had said. "In a thousand years, who knows what magic will exist?"

They had left a note with the box. Uncle Marco had the best handwriting, so he wrote it out, in three languages—*This*

*box contains an evil creature. It will steal the magic of paintings.
Do not allow it to escape. This is proof against it.*

And Rosa had drawn her very best radish at the bottom.

It was sealed in a little metal tube, stoppered with wax, on fine parchment. Artists knew how to make things that would stand the test of time.

Just in case, though, Aunt Nadia and Uncle Alfonso had taken turns painting a new crow on the box, standing atop a fanged radish. But they did not use the enchanted charcoal, and this one did not come to life.

Payne had argued that they should throw the whole thing into a bonfire, Scarling and all, and end the threat forever.

"It'll end you, too," said Rosa. "You said that if the Scarling burns up, everything its charcoal created burns too. We're *not* going to do that."

The crow swallowed. "It might be worth it," he said. "To make sure it never comes back again."

"There will be *no* heroic sacrifices in the studio," snapped Grandmama. "I will *not* allow it!"

"Besides," said Aunt Nadia, stirring her coffee with a palette knife, "if you weren't around, we might have silverware again, and I, for one, wouldn't know how to act."

So there was no bonfire. Instead they all stood together around the hole, late one night. Sergio and Uncle Alfonso brought bags of concrete and Aunt Nadia poured the water. The rest of the Studio Mandolini—and one young member of Studio Magnifico—held hands and watched as the painted crow vanished under the weight of poured stone.

If anyone noticed the next day that there was already a bit of concrete at the bottom of the hole, they didn't mention it. They just backed the cart up and filled it in the rest of the way, nearly two tons worth, to set a proper foundation for the fountain.

And that was that.

"I was jealous at first," said Serena abruptly.

Rosa looked at her, surprised.

"That you could make the illuminations come to life," said her friend.

"Oh," said Rosa. And then, "It wasn't good, really. I made them, but the scribblings kept destroying them. It isn't fair to make something just so somebody else can stomp on it. I wouldn't have done it if it wasn't so important." She sighed. She still felt guilty about the radishes.

Serena nodded. "Yeah. I figured that out." She nudged Rosa's ribs. "It wasn't your fault."

"I know." The problem was that *knowing* and *feeling* were two different things. Rosa scuffed at the ground with her toe. "And I was jealous of your commission and you were jealous of Nadia's painting and—"

"There's a lot of jealousy to go around," said Serena. "I guess as long as we're not trying to kill each other with giant charcoal monsters because of it, we're doing okay."

Rosa snorted. "Aunt Nadia would say that's a low bar to clear."

Serena grinned. "I've decided I'm going to be proud instead. After all, you can make living illuminations, which is amazing, and you're my friend, so I must be at least a little amazing too, right?"

This struck Rosa as extremely sensible, even if she wasn't going to make any more live illuminations if she could help it.

They still had the charcoal, back at the studio. Rosa hadn't been remotely tempted to use it.

There was still one lone radish drawing. It was the elephant-nosed one. They found it, battered but intact, inside Uncle Marco's studio. It had been defending Walter the beetle.

Rosa was glad it had made it. It didn't seem unhappy. It spent most of its time with Walter. They had made friends, insomuch as a beetle and an enchanted drawing could be friends.

She shook herself, trying to shake off the melancholy mood. They'd won. Everybody was still alive. Cousin Sergio had a scar on his forehead, but he didn't seem to mind. Rosa wasn't actually sure if he'd noticed. Aunt Nadia was still a little shaky on her bad knee, but she'd finished off the angel painting, sitting on one of Uncle Marco's wheeled stools. The Merchant Guild had paid handsomely for it and the Baker's Guild was already asking if she was available for another.

Payne was the one who had changed the most. He didn't seem as bossy, or as confident. He still stole spoons and commented on paintings, but sometimes he would perch on the walls for long, quiet hours, looking at nothing. Once or twice, Rosa found him in Sergio's bay, staring down at the art history book, at the paintings that Tybalt had made hundreds of years ago.

She didn't know what to say to make things better. Uncle Alfonso had told her that there wasn't anything to say. "It's easy when bad people die," he told her. "And it's not easy when good people die, but at least it's straightforward, and you know exactly how you're supposed to feel. But when someone who was good and bad dies, someone you loved, but who hurt you... then you don't know how to feel at all. If you're sad, it feels wrong, and if you're not sad, that feels wrong too."

"That seems complicated," said Rosa. "And hard."

"People are hard," Uncle Alfonso agreed. "Grief is hard, too."

"Everything is hard!" said Rosa, falling over on the couch in despair.

"Particularly locating stuffed armadillos," her uncle said mournfully. "Speaking of which, I don't suppose you've...? No." He sighed. "Perhaps you and Payne can look for it together."

"Will that help?"

"It's bound to. Hunting stuffed armadillos is a well-known cure for moping." Her uncle tapped the side of his nose and nodded solemnly. Rosa rolled her eyes.

As if the memory had summoned him, Payne landed on the ground in front of Rosa and Serena. He had a piece of silver ribbon in his beak.

"Sooo shiny," he said happily. He looked more cheerful than he had in weeks, waving the ribbon back and forth.

"I suppose it's better than silverware," said Rosa.

"I got it off a *hat!*"

Rosa and Serena looked at Payne, then at each other. Then they both began to laugh.

Arm in arm, the two young illuminators walked back toward the Studio Mandolini, while the painted crow flew over their heads, trailing a ribbon of silver behind him.

ACKNOWLEDGMENTS

I seem to have a bad habit of writing kid books, selling them, and then what with one thing and another, through no fault of anyone involved, the book ends up not getting published and I get it back. It happened with *Wizard's Guide* and here we are again with *Illuminations*. (Ironically, I wrote this as a replacement for *Wizard's Guide*...and here we are. Again.)

The odd dates scattered through the manuscript are derived from the French Revolutionary Calendar, a very peculiar calendar created in the aftermath of the French Revolution, to remove all traces of mythology, Roman emperors, and other things deemed non-revolutionary. In our world, it didn't last very long—I fear it's not actually a very good calendar—but it's delightful and rather absurd, full of things like "Turnip Day" and "Compost Day." I loved all the imagery and was always looking for some piece of writing to use it. (You can still buy the French Revolutionary Calendar online, and never miss Turnip Day again!)

Paynes Gray is a real color, an extremely deep blue-black. I thought it would be a fine color for a crow.

Anyway! Much love to my publishers at Argyll, my patient editor K.B. Spangler, and my copyeditors Cassie and Jes. More love to my agent Helen, who got the manuscript back after some years in limbo, and most love of all to my husband Kevin, who has been with me through more books than I can count.

T. Kingfisher,
North Carolina
October 2022

ABOUT THE AUTHOR

T. Kingfisher is the vaguely absurd pen-name of Ursula Vernon, an author from North Carolina. In another life, she writes children's books and weird comics. She has been nominated for the World Fantasy and the Eisner, and has won the Hugo, Sequoyah, Nebula, Alfie, WSFA, Cóyotl and Ursa Major awards, as well as a half-dozen Junior Library Guild selections.

This is the name she uses when writing things for grown-ups, although I grant you, some of them are actually kid's books, because branding is hard. Her work includes horror, epic fantasy, fairy-tale retellings and odd little stories about elves and goblins.

When she is not writing, she is probably out in the garden, trying to make eye contact with butterflies.

twitter.com/ursulav

patreon.com/ursulav

ALSO BY T. KINGFISHER

As T. Kingfisher

A Wizard's Guide To Defensive Baking

Paladin's Grace

Paladin's Strength

Paladin's Hope

Swordheart

Clockwork Boys

The Wonder Engine

Minor Mage

Nine Goblins

Toad Words & Other Stories

The Seventh Bride

The Raven & The Reindeer

Bryony & Roses

Jackalope Wives & Other Stories

Summer in Orcus

From Tor:

Nettle & Bone

What Moves The Dead

From Saga:

The Twisted Ones

The Hollow Places

As Ursula Vernon

From Sofawolf Press:

Black Dogs Duology

House of Diamond

Mountain of Iron

Digger

It Made Sense At The Time

For kids:

Nurk

Dragonbreath Series

Hamster Princess Series

Castle Hangnail

Milton Keynes UK
Ingram Content Group UK Ltd.
UKHW041608050524
442244UK00008B/116